VICTORIOUS SWORDS
BOOK THREE OF THE DURLINDRATH SERIES

Robert Ryan

Cover Design by www.bookcoverartistry.com

ISBN-13 978-0-9942054-5-2
(print edition)

Trotting Fox Press

I0458220

Contents

1. Two Futures   3
2. The Call to Serve   9
3. Old as the Bones of the Earth   16
4. The Fire of the Sun   23
5. A Dark Shadow   30
6. Relentless Swords   35
7. All the Days of Your Life   40
8. The World Shall Tremble   45
9. More than You Seem   51
10. Strife and Mayhem   55
11. Now is Our Chance   62
12. Strange things are Abroad   66
13. Hilk Var Jernik   71
14. A Great Honor   81
15. Like a Spear   86
16. If Only I could See   90
17. All Dead Men, Now   95
18. Something Stirs   99
19. They Will Tell their Children   103
20. Tall and Terrible   110
21. The Future is not Fixed   114
22. Stealth   120
23. Why do they Wait?   131
24. Have I not the Right?   138
25. The Light Grows Brighter   142
26. The Storm Breaks   145
27. Burn!   152
28. Filled with Power   161
29. Can You Deny Her?   167
Epilogue   177
Encyclopedic Glossary   182

1. Two Futures

Brand, his heart thrashing, ran to Kareste. Pain showed on her every feature, and tears of anguish glistened on her pale cheeks. She had fallen, and he went to help, as he knew he always would.

She trembled at his touch, but she was alive. And that thought nearly overwhelmed him, for he did not know what he would do if she died.

Her eyes, once green-gold, flickered open. There was now a shadow in them, and it was one of more than pain. The sorcery that she had invoked, the power that had run through her, had been beyond her strength to bear. But she *had* borne it, and such an act based on willpower alone, disregarding the weakness of the flesh, would have consequences.

He sensed the sorcery of the staff. Shurilgar's staff. A thing of ancient power beyond comprehension. The remnant of its unleashing still charged the air. Its lingering force was everywhere. And he saw it even in her eyes. What had her use of it cost her?

She shuddered violently, and then stilled. With her eyes half lidded, she spoke in a ragged whisper.

"You turn your back on the beasts?"

"You need me," he replied, "and I'm here."

She opened her eyes wider. "Foolish boy. But it's well for you," she added, "that I kept to my word."

She struggled to sit up a little higher. He helped her, and then she spoke more strongly.

"Behold! The Halathrin are free!"

For the first time, he turned to look. And what he saw amazed him.

They stood there, free of the forms of the beasts that had trapped them. They were gathered in a group, and a faint shimmer of white light was about them. Some were golden haired, but most had hair of a strange silver-white. It was more than blond. And the shimmer about them seemed as though the light of the full moon had been caught and refined, and it spilled from them in the same way that mist rose from the surface of a lake.

They were mostly men, but there were several women among them. One of these was the first that he had seen a little while ago. She looked back over her shoulder at him, but did not speak.

He turned to Kareste again. "Are you alright?"

She shifted position, trying to get comfortable. "I don't know. I feel strange."

He put his arm around her, helping her to sit upright. Shurilgar's staff lay on the ground between them. They both saw it, but neither of them said anything.

"I'll get you some water," he offered.

He walked over to the horses. There, he retrieved a waterbag and brought it back. He helped her hold it in her trembling hands while she drank.

When she was done, she gazed at him silently. He still saw pain in her eyes, and anguish. There was uncertainty too, and then, as though she cast a veil over her face, it was all gone. The lòhren inscrutability had returned, and she showed nothing of how she felt. So it always was with her. She hid her emotions out of habit, and he only caught glimpses at unguarded moments. Now, it seemed, she wished to hide them more than ever.

The staff remained between them, the unspoken question of what they each wanted to do with it hung in the air. And they both ignored it for the moment. Neither of them was ready to raise that subject.

There was a stir behind them. The Halathrin appeared to have come to a decision about something, and the girl he had seen before came over to him. He saw relief on her face.

It was no surprise that she also seemed buoyant with a great joy. She was freed from the sorcery that had trapped her in the form of a beast. But then he remembered that Kareste had said the beasts were real as well, that the Halathrin had been joined *to* them.

His gaze darted around, and it quickly found what he sought. There were some twenty bodies beyond the Halathrin, back near the trees. They were misshapen things, twisted and fur clad, and he could only see them dimly. He was glad of that. But even as he watched, their dark forms faded into greasy smoke that drifted sluggishly away.

The girl stood before him. "Who are you?" she asked.

"My name's Brand. I'm bodyguard to the king of Cardoroth."

She looked with her clear-sighted gaze into his eyes, and then slowly shook her head.

"Nay, gentle Brand. That's merely your name and one of your tasks. It's not who you are."

He felt uncomfortable, for he had a sense that her mind perceived more of him than his could of her. She looked at him, but she saw more than was visible to the eye.

"Then, lady, who am I?"

She shook her head once more and there was a little shimmer of light as though a candle wavered in an otherwise unfelt breeze.

"Much I could say, but I will say naught. It is for you to discover, and the discovering will shape you. I dare not interfere."

"I've had many foretell my future," he answered. "Some with accuracy, but not yet has one with foresight *not* told me what they saw, accurate or otherwise."

"Foresight?" she said, with a little tilt of her head. "I don't know what you mean. I cannot see the future. I have not that power, else the elùgroth would not have caught me in his sorcery."

She shuddered, and a darkness dimmed her beautiful features.

"I see only the present," she continued, "but mayhap I see it clearly, and the present casts a shadow forward in time. You don't need to see the full length of a late afternoon tree-shadow to know the tree's shape – the living thing itself tells you that."

Brand did not understand, but he had no opportunity to question her because the other Halathrin were coming over.

They gave graceful bows, but did not speak. It seemed the girl was their spokesperson. She gave him her own little curtsey, and then straightened.

"My name is Harlinlanloth."

She turned her gaze away from Brand, and he saw a flicker of doubt in her eyes.

"Who is the girl that freed us? I would speak with her."

"Kareste," Brand answered. He turned around to look at his companion. She seemed to be recovering, but only a very little. It would take her days, perhaps weeks, to recuperate fully.

The girl curtseyed once again. It was a deft movement of sublime grace.

"You chose wisely," she said.

6

Brand could not decide if her voice was like velvet or steel.

Kareste answered, her own voice weak but edged with a curt tone that he knew well.

"How so?"

"If you had used the power of the staff for domination, to turn us into your slaves and to usurp the control of the elùgroths with your own, the power within the staff would instead own you. You mastered temptation, and therefore mastered the staff, at least this once. But the question has become this. What will you do now?"

Brand thought it was a good question. But it was not the only one. Now that the Halathrin were free, would they not wish to preserve the staff whose timber was sacred to them? And if so, what was he to do? He had no heart to fight them, or to fight Kareste. And yet he *must* destroy the staff.

Also, what of the power within him? He had freed it, and in doing so it lit up the path laid out ahead of him. To be sure, he did not seem to see his future as clearly as the Halathrin girl had done, but he saw it nonetheless.

His destiny was to become a lòhren. To serve the land. The magic inside him made it so, and he felt the connection. Yet magic was a thing that he distrusted, and all the more so now.

These matters were not all, either. Over and above them, calling to him from his childhood, was the voice of his own people. His responsibility as a lòhren would be to the whole land and not just a small and faraway community of little consequence to others. Even if it was everything to him.

He saw before him two futures, two separate paths. He wanted one, and not the other. But would fate allow him to choose?

He did not think so. He had been put on the path of a lòhren at every step of this quest, since perhaps even long before. Every move he had made, though he had not had any alternative, had brought him to this point. He had a feeling that it would continue, and that troubled him. It troubled him more than even an elùgroth, for the thought of becoming a lòhren *scared* him.

2. The Call to Serve

They were all gathered around Kareste. Harlinlanloth's words hung in the air, but whether or not Kareste believed them was another matter.

Slowly, Kareste reached for the staff. Brand wondered if he should have taken it before, while he could. Kareste had been true to her word and freed the Halathrin from the sorcery that bound them to the beasts, but did she have the strength to destroy the thing that gave her so much power?

She clasped the staff and used it to help her stand. Brand wanted to help, but he knew that reaching out toward her could be seen as an attempt to take the staff itself. That might be all that was needed to tip her thoughts in the wrong direction.

Kareste stood on wobbly legs, and she leaned on the broken staff. Unexpectedly, Brand thought of Aranloth. How many times had he seen the lòhren stand just so? But Aranloth's choices were made long ago. With Kareste, anything was still possible.

There was determination on her face that Brand had not seen before. She had always been strong willed, but a decision of one kind or another now seemed graven on her face as an image was onto stone.

She looked at them all, and though she was travel stained and dirty, though she was spent from their long journey and exhausted from the latest fight, he had never seen her look more beautiful. But the shadow was still in her eyes, and they seemed dark to him. He could not glimpse even a fraction of what she thought.

Then she turned her gaze directly on him as though the Halathrin were not there. She blinked a few times, and then she shrugged.

Brand watched her, uncertain. The Halathrin seemed calm, but underneath their exterior he sensed enormous tension.

Kareste stirred, and then spoke. "My choice is made. I promised Brand that I would destroy the staff, and I don't care what Durletha thought," she pointed at the witch's body, "I have power, and I *will* have more, for there are many things wrong in the land that need righting. But I will not achieve it with Shurilgar's staff. Even now, I fight its lure. If it isn't destroyed, and destroyed soon, I'll succumb."

The Halathrin looked at her gravely. After a few moments, Harlinlanloth spoke.

"It is so with you and your kind. But it is not so with us. The staff is a sacred thing. Long we protected its other half, hid it from the world, revered the memory of who once, long ago even to us, was lost. We could do so again, for we seek not to use its powers. We are not tempted."

Brand turned to the Halathrin girl.

"You know that there's another half, but do you know how it's used? How it's used even as we speak?"

Harlinlanloth looked at him with troubled eyes.

"Nay," she answered. "Only that the elùgroths possess it."

"Then I shall tell you. It's used in a siege. The enemy encircles Cardoroth City. Elugs, and all manner of other dark things, including elùgroths, draw on its dark power. The staff that is sacred to you is used by them to break down the city's defenses. Brave soldiers, and brave lòhrens, die to protect what they love. And though they fight, though they fight to their last breath, yet still the enemy will overcome them. At least, while the enemy wields the power of the staff."

He paused, allowing an opportunity for consideration of his words, before he went on.

"Even Aranloth cannot defy such power forever. It may already be too late, for long have Kareste and I tarried when we could have destroyed the staff earlier. And as you no doubt know, to destroy the one half is to destroy the other, for the power that infused it, when it was one, binds it still as two. Cardoroth may so be saved, and not only that, but great evil could be prevented that otherwise would follow as surely you know it must, so long as the power remains in the possession of the elùgroths. I don't wish to cause you, you who have been through so much, distress. But the staff must be destroyed. Not just for the sake of Kareste, not just for my sake, not just for Cardoroth, but for the whole land."

When Brand ceased speaking, there was silence. It was perhaps the longest speech he had ever made, and he thought he could have done better. But at least his thoughts were in the open. But how the Halathrin would react to them, he did not know.

The bulk of the Halathrin seemed ready to speak, but the girl silenced them with a slight gesture of her hand. She, it appeared, was their leader.

"This is no small thing for us," Harlinlanloth said. "We must speak amongst ourselves for a while."

She looked at Brand, and though he could not read her intentions, he saw sympathy in her eyes.

"Yet I hear you," she continued. "There's truth in your heart, and I sense it in your words. But this is a choice as even the wise should dread to make. On the one hand is the risk to Alithoras – on the other the veneration of one who is no longer alive, and yet who, while he lived, gave all he had, even the ultimate sacrifice, to protect the land."

11

She shook her head slowly. "To destroy the last remembrance of him is a dishonor beyond endurance to those who saw his deeds and heard his words. And most of my kind are accounted among that number. To them, in the end, I must justify my actions."

Brand did not answer. Instead, he gave a small bow. He understood what she said, and she understood the argument he had made. Nothing else needed saying, not yet, at least. And he hoped it never would.

The Halathrin withdrew. They gathered beneath the shadows of the nearby fringe of trees. They were close enough that Brand could hear the murmur of their voices, but not so close that he could understand them. But he did not wish to listen in anyway; theirs was a private conversation about things that he would never be able to truly understand.

He mused on his feelings. The power that was in him had been woken, and there was no way to cause it to slumber again. It was like a fire; having been sparked to life it must burn. He could not turn it back any more than a flower could refuse to bloom when the heat of approaching summer warmed the earth. Its time had come.

He closed his eyes and felt what he had sensed for some time: the need of the land. The land, from whence all power and life ultimately came. It called to him. He felt its demand to serve. It was the call that rumor and legend from everywhere in Alithoras claimed lòhrens heard. He knew it now for the truth.

But what of the Duthenor? What of the usurper who ruled in place of his father? Small things perhaps in the greater scheme of the world, in the face of the vast threat to Alithoras. But not to him. Could he heed a call, no matter how just and right, when his heart yearned for something else, equally just and right in its own way? Did he have the power to refuse the call? If he did, *should* he?

These also were questions that even the wise would dread to make. To serve without belief, without power of will and conviction of heart, was not to serve at all. It would only open the door to defeat, for the enemy would take such weakness and use it ruthlessly as a tool for their victory.

And yet there was no real way to refuse the call. The land outweighed all else. But why *him*? He did not believe in fate, did not believe that the future was set in stone. Let the land call another who could better answer! Yet who was that?

Brand's mind began to reel. He had no answers, was not even sure if he was asking the right questions. Perhaps he should run. If he were fast, if he fled far away, perhaps he could outrun them. And that thought became suddenly strong, for as he considered what would happen if he did that, he perceived with greater clarity the great shadow of the tasks that lay ahead of him. And even the hint of them was daunting. It was a mighty destiny, but not what his heart wanted. He steeled himself with an iron will: first, he must see things through with the staff.

Kareste, as always, sensed his mood. More importantly, she perceived his doubts, and was as direct as always.

"We don't need them to destroy the staff," she said. "If we must, we can do it while they talk."

Brand studied her for a moment. "Haven't *you* had a change of heart."

"Don't make light of it. I know now better than everyone the power in this thing." She gripped the staff tightly. "And the temptation. It would lead anyone into evil, into the very heart of darkness. It must be destroyed, whether the Halathrin will it or no. Aranloth should have seen to it when he had the chance long ago. And I'll do it now, while I still have the will to do so."

"Maybe so," he answered. "But I don't think either of us have the power to burn it. Lòhrengai will not obliterate elùgai, and to try to do it that way is only going to bring the power within it into opposition. It couldn't be done quickly either, and then you'd have some very upset Halathrin to deal with." He paused, looking over at them thoughtfully. "The deed needs their cooperation, if we can get it. They see the thing as something different from what we do. And if we can get their cooperation, it will need much timber and a great fire. As I said, I wouldn't care to invoke lòhrengai to destroy it. That is to open yourself up to the staff itself, for such power can go both ways, and who knows how the power within it would react?"

She tilted her head. "I hadn't thought of that. Do you really think it's possible?"

"I don't know. You're more learned by far than I in such matters. But I think in truth that few ever walked the land who understood the powers of one of the great masters such as Shurilgar. Besides all of that, the Halathrin deserve better."

"Maybe so," she said. "But people rarely get what they deserve."

He did not answer that, and she shrugged. "Anyway, it was a thought. We'll do it your way, but I hope you can read these people better than I can. I have no idea what they'll do from one moment to the next."

Brand gave his own shrug. "Me neither, but as I always seem to have to do, I'll trust to my luck. I think they'll agree."

Kareste raise an eyebrow. "You have more than your fair share of luck. But we'll see. One day it'll run out. I just hope it isn't today."

She stopped talking, and he knew why. The Halathrin were returning.

"But it might be," she whispered a moment later under her breath.

3. Old as the Bones of the Earth

The Halathrin approached. Their visage was stern, and their eyes glinted with steady determination. It was the unwavering glance of immortals who endured through time, and the force of their will was honed by the long years so that their mind, once decided on some course, was not easily swayed.

There was a shimmer about them. It was stronger than before, for now that they seemed to have some purpose the power that was in them was focused. Just what they could do, and how strong they were in body and mind, Brand could not tell. But their powers were greater than that of human kind.

He felt tempted to draw his sword. This might yet become a fight, though he was still not sure if he could do that. He was sick of killing, but he began to feel that deep down inside him the urge to fight for Cardoroth, and for those who had placed their trust in him, was still there.

He waited, stony faced. He could not read them, but he was confident that they could not read him either.

Harlinlanloth came to stand before him. She was tall and proud. A light burned in her eyes, and though he could not read her, he knew this at least: her spirit was as proud as her manner, and though she was a gentle soul, there was also a fire in her that once woken would flare and burn and consume. As an enemy, she would be implacable. As a friend, loyal to death.

His heart pounded loudly, for he sensed in her a kindred spirit. But he betrayed no outward sign of his emotion.

Harlinlanloth stood still and looked at him intently. "Know this," she said with quiet force. "This decision is not easy for us. The wood of the staff comes from a sacred grove of elms in our forest realm. That alone makes it more precious than you can understand. But the trees grew on a mound, the burial place of our great king who led us to these shores during our exodus, for the Halathrin do not entomb their dead in stone as is the custom among men. It was from one of those sacred trees that Shurilgar stole the timber for his staff."

She paused. All was quiet about them. The hills were gray ghosts and the tarn silent as death.

"Yet we are not unaware that afterward the staff was possessed of an evil power. Yet still it remains a token of the living tree and the rest of the grove that Shurilgar razed by fire and elùgai. The staff alone, though broken in two, is all that remains of our memorial. For still no grass grows nor any flower or tree on the flame-blackened mound. You could never understand what a sad sight that is to us."

"Lady," he answered softly, "I understand death and tragedy."

She did not look away. "But you don't understand the bearing of it through years uncounted." She paused thoughtfully and then continued, a hesitant tone in her voice. "Though one day you will." She took a deep breath and went on with greater certainty. "So much of our story you may already know. Aranloth knows it, and it is clear that he set you on the path of this quest. But what you don't know is this."

The Halathrin girl swept her arm out imperiously behind her to indicate the other Halathrin.

"We are twenty," she said. "We are always twenty, for once there were twenty trees. We are the Drinhalath, the preservers of what was lost, the memory keepers and the

17

guardians of the little that remains. Our lives are pledged to guard it. And in truth, we have no power or authority to agree or disagree with what you want. That is a decision for our king and his counselors. And yet," she said slowly, "a decision must be made, and made now else it will come too late for your people. And maybe ours also, for out in the world it may be that we cannot preserve our charge. So it proved in our own realm. We could not protect it there. And under our laws, the decision falls to me."

Brand felt for her. There was a hint of doubt in her eyes, of the anguish that she hid. For it was an impossible choice that she must make. And he knew what that was like.

"I lead the Drinhalath," she said. "The decision rests with me. Know this!"

Her voice changed, and he sensed that a sudden decision lay behind it.

"Our ways are not your ways, and there are consequences for any choice I make. But though we're different, the last remnant of sacred wood is as precious to us as your people are to you. We love what we love, and for us the memory of a loved one does not fade. For we who are immortal live longer and deeper in the past than those who live more briefly."

Kareste stirred and might have spoken, but Harlinlanloth went on.

"I don't mean to say that you love less, only that experience with your kind has taught us our differences. We live in the past as much as the present, and our thought encompasses both at the same time."

She paused a moment, and then shifted her gaze back to Brand.

"Know this, also. The Halathrin have long guessed where Aranloth secured the second half of the staff. That place is far away from here. You could have destroyed it there, but rather you came here to free us, at risk to yourselves and with the risk of delay to your people. We're in your debt, and we take such matters seriously."

Harlinlanloth bowed again, and so now did every Halathrin behind her. This, Brand noticed, was a deeper bow, as graceful as their every other movement, but somehow more formal this time. There was something behind Harlinlanloth's words that he could not quite grasp.

She straightened and spoke again. "We are in your debt, and as you made sacrifices for us, we will make them for you. The staff will burn."

There were tears in her eyes as she spoke, and a catch in her voice that tore at his heart.

"Lady," Brand said, "I would that it were not so."

"It is what it is," she answered, "And sometimes wishing is in vain. Yet still do we appreciate your thoughts. And though the staff must be destroyed, we would do so with dignity and in memory of he whom it commemorates."

Brand nodded. "How shall it be done?"

"There are funerary rites that are important to us. We would perform them."

Brand did not answer, but bowed in accession.

The next little while was solemn. In silence they each collected what dry timber they could. This they stacked into a large bier. After some time, it stood waist high and stretched out in a square with each side twice the length of a man. When it burned, Brand knew, it would burn with great intensity. And that was well, for though it was made of wood, he did not think Shurilgar's staff would catch fire easily.

Harlinlanloth approached Kareste. Gently, she reached out for the staff. Kareste gave it to her, and though her

19

face betrayed no sign of struggle, Brand sensed that it took much force of will to pass it over.

Harlinlanloth laid the talisman gently on top of the bier, and then the Halathrin stood around it. Brand and Kareste stood back a little way, and watched in silence.

Harlinlanloth led the Halathrin in some sort of chant. Brand could not pick up the words at first, for it seemed to him that while it was the Halathrin tongue, there were many words and phrases that he had not heard before and he could not guess their meaning. Yet one phrase he understood: *Eleth nar duril.* This the Halathrin repeated frequently – lie in peace.

Kareste whispered to him, for evidently she understood more than he, or had learned of this rite from the lòhrens.

"They invoke the blessings of the sun and moon, of the sky and grass, of the forest and field. They seek oneness with all that was and all that will be, and they speak to the spirit of the departed, asking him to lie in peace, to be one with the universe as they will after him. They ask him to wait in tranquility until they are joined again, and the broken is mended, and the lost is found."

Brand was not sure what to make of it. But he saw the expression on the faces of the Halathrin, and whatever he thought did not matter. They believed, and it was a moment of great emotion for them. No matter that Halath, king of the Halathrin, had died thousands of years ago. It seemed to him that they felt his death as keenly now as they must have on that very first day. Immortality, perhaps, was not so great as people made out.

The chanting continued without cessation, yet one of the Halathrin peeled away at some sign that Brand did not see. The warrior walked in stately fashion, stepping in time to the sonorous chanting. Soon, he plucked a handful of willow leaves that hung over the tarn. He returned,

20

stepping in the same manner, and as he came to the bier he scattered the leaves over its top.

Before the warrior finished, another of the Halathrin peeled away. He also marched in the same fashion, yet his pace was slower, and the chanting became even more deliberate and deeper.

This warrior stooped and gathered soil from the edge of the tarn in his hands. It was dark and loamy, enriched be years of uncounted leaf falls.

The man returned. With graceful movements he spread the soil over the bier. And even as he did so, Harlinlanloth was already moving. Hers was a grace beyond even the others. She moved at a pace so stately, so elegant, that she barely seemed to move at all, and Brand could not take his gaze off her. There were tears on her cheeks, but her eyes shone with determination, and her voice did not falter.

The Halathrin girl reached the tarn. She ignored leaf and soil. Instead, she bent, scooped the dark water into her cupped hands, and stood again all in one fluid motion.

She returned to the others. Not one drop of water was spilled, and then with a sudden movement she cast the water over the bier. It glistened on the staff. The Halathrin chanting rose to a higher pitch, and it gathered pace. The ceremony, symbolizing many things beyond Brand's comprehension, was obviously drawing near its end.

The chanting was now high and remote. He understood little of it, but there was a beauty in its sound that transfixed him. He realized that the words and the rite were old; old even to the immortals. That was why he could not understand it, even though he spoke their tongue. It was a part of their heritage so ancient that it no doubt preceded their coming to Alithoras. It was old as the bones of the earth beneath their feet, and it meant something to these people that he could never understand. It was ancient even to them, bringing to life a language that they spoke eons ago in a land beyond the shores of Alithoras.

Unexpectedly, there was a slight falter in the chant. Brand looked to Kareste, and he saw that she was uneasy. And she did not look at the Halathrin, but out into the woods. Whatever had disturbed the immortals had disturbed her, and then he remembered the words of Durletha just before she died: *I will have the staff now, even if I must kill you, for others come for it...*

4. The Fire of the Sun

Gilhain stood atop the battlement. The noon heat beat down, and the sky was bright. He grinned to himself. He knew that he should not, not amidst such terrible waste of life, yet he did.

Shorty had been his champion and had defeated Hvargil. He had also escaped the sorcerers. This was a set of events to bring chagrin to the enemy, and what displeased them was good for Cardoroth – and his sense of humor.

He stood a moment longer, enjoying the feeling. There was satisfaction in being able to do so, but soon he must turn his mind toward facing the next threat, whatever it would be. Certainly, there would be more attacks, more elugs coming against the wall, but what else?

Aranloth was beside him, and he spoke into the silence. It seemed to Gilhain that the lòhren uncannily read his thoughts.

"Who knows what the enemy will do now?" he said. "They've been rebuffed, but not beaten. They'll come against you again, but they won't do so in the same way twice."

Lornach and Taingern were there also. They looked at each other, but only Taingern spoke.

"We'll be ready," he said.

They were simple words, but Gilhain felt the force of will that lay behind them. It was in the way the two men stood also, for they were warriors and they were riding high on confidence. They looked like they could proceed through the gate and take on the enemy just by themselves.

Gilhain understood the feeling, but he knew it would not last. He put an arm around each of their shoulders and stood between them. Together, they looked out over the battlement.

Aranloth stood a little apart, but he leaned against a merlon and looked out also. But though the lòhren's eyes gazed in that direction, Gilhain knew that he was not contemplating the enemy, but rather Brand. Where was he? What was he doing? Gilhain knew those same questions very well; he had asked them often enough himself.

There was no attack as yet, and it seemed that there was no sign of one building, either. Gilhain dropped his arms from the shoulders of the two Durlin and sighed.

"This is a good time for me to walk along the battlement and give some heart to the men, if I can."

"You always do," Lornach said. "More than you know."

They strolled along the battlement. They went slowly, for it was an oppressively hot day. The other Durlin, those who remained alive, joined them. And even Aranloth trailed along, a frown on his face and apparently deep in thought.

They came to an archer restringing his bow. "How goes it, friend?" Gilhain asked.

The man gave a slight smile. "Well, your Majesty. The light is good, and I have plenty of arrows."

Gilhain clapped him on the back. "Well spoken. If only you had an arrow for every enemy in the host and the time to shoot them all."

"Have them line up for me," the archer said with a straight face, "and I'll oblige you, Sire."

Gilhain gave him a wink. "Watch them closely," he answered. "And I'll see what I can do."

They moved on. Gilhain spoke to anyone and everyone as he walked the Cardurleth. Most of the soldiers merely listened though, for these were quiet and grim men. It was usually only the extroverts who spoke to him, and that was fine by him. These were the people who made jokes and lightened the mood. The others need not join in to benefit from that. Morale was like a fire: it was either sparking to life or dying. Only rarely did it burn steadily. And Gilhain knew it was his job to keep it burning, to keep it burning against the dark.

On they went, and Gilhain had spoken to a great many before he turned around and started to head back toward the rampart above the gate: his normal spot from which to direct the defense. He stopped and talked just as frequently as he had on the way out, and there was much grim banter. He took extra time for those who manned the Cardurleth despite a wound, yet who had chosen to remain with their regiment on the wall.

Gilhain had met all types of soldiers: the steely eyed, the mentally scared who joked to hide it, those who cared neither for life nor death but rather sought oblivion after some personal tragedy. He had met them all, talked to them all and understood them all. For he was at times all those things himself.

They eventually came back to the archer. His bow was long since restrung. Now, he was inspecting his arrows, checking their heads and shafts and red fletching.

The king nodded to him. "Those are long shafts," he said.

"Aye," the archer answered. "But I have long arms and the bow is well-matched to me."

"How far can you fire?"

The archer considered the question for a moment.

"With these arrows, close on three hundred yards."

"And how far can you shoot with accuracy?"

"That's a different thing altogether. Perhaps a third as far, depending on conditions."

Gilhain rubbed his chin. "That's further and more accurate than most."

The archer grinned at him. "I'm a tall man, and strong. I've been shooting since my youth, and there have been times when I went hungry if I missed. That sort of thing teaches a man to shoot well."

"I don't doubt it," Gilhain said. He looked out speculatively at the enemy host. "You could land an arrow among them?" he asked.

"I could, but at that range it would do very little damage."

"True," Gilhain said. "But should you see an elùgroth somewhere in the front ranks, it might be worth the attempt. If you strike one thus, there's ten gold pieces in it for you."

The archer grinned. "I'll see what I can do."

"Good man."

Gilhain looked out at the enemy again. They were not quite so far away that the archer faced an impossible challenge. Yet it was very nearly so.

He paused where he was a moment, studying the host. Something seemed to be happening among it, for there was movement in its center. But the host was so massive that he could not really see anything that far away. It waited there impatiently, a dark mass commanded by its dark masters. From both sides it stretched out wings to encircle the whole city. But Cardoroth was large, and those wings were stretched thin. They were not for attack but merely to ensure no one left or entered the city.

Gilhain gave a small sigh. How many times had he studied the host? And how many times had he found a weakness? But it did not matter, he would keep on looking and thinking. And even if he found no weakness, then this much at least he could be grateful for: the enemy did not build and employ siege engines. They did not use them in their homeland, either among the elugs or Azan. The land was not suitable, being mostly mountainous and rough. Nor were there walled cities. And anyway, they preferred to fight just as they did here. The elùgroths took pleasure in it, and they worked their soldiers up into a mad frenzy. Sometimes, Gilhain thought, they would attack the wall with nothing but hands and teeth if their masters asked them to.

There was movement along the rampart, and then Arell was there. She gave Gilhain a quick curtsey. "Your Majesty," she said. Then, she pointed her finger firmly at Lornach. "*You*," she continued. "You haven't come by for your examination as you said you would. Are you a fool? Do you know what sort of injuries you may have sustained in your fight with Hvargil? Do you know that some injuries are internal and not apparent straight away?"

He started to speak, but she cut straight through whatever he would have said.

"Don't bother to answer that. I *know* you know. I've told you these things myself often enough."

She turned to Gilhain. "This is unacceptable. I'm responsible for treating any injuries to the Durlin, but I can't treat them if they don't cooperate."

Gilhain turned to the short man. "Well, Lornach, why haven't you done as she requested? It seems to me that there are very good reasons for what she asks."

Lornach gave the healer a hard look, but it did not fool Gilhain. He knew the bond that was between Arell and all the Durlin, Brand especially.

"My lord, as it happens, I *did* report to her for an examination."

Gilhain glanced at Arell. "Is that so?"

Arell snorted. "If by report for an examination he means that he rolled his eyes at me, pointed to his arms and legs and said 'all still here,' before walking off, then yes, he's been examined. I wanted more than *that* though." She returned Lornach's stare. "But he pleaded that he must report to you directly. I only let him go after he promised to come straight back. But he never did."

Lornach clapped a hand to his forehead. "That reminds me, my lord." He pulled from a pocket in his white surcoat the cloth belt Gilhain had given him to wear as his champion. "This is yours, Sire."

He reached out to give the cloth to Gilhain.

"Don't change the subject, Shorty. You can keep the cloth – you may need it again someday. But for now, go along with Arell. You know she's right."

Lornach tucked the band of cloth away again. "But Sire, she lectures me all the time on what to eat and how to exercise and—"

"More likely," Gilhain interrupted him, "she tells you not to drink so much beer."

Lornach pretended to look surprised at the comment, but the answer he was going to give died in his throat and a sudden wariness came into his eyes.

Gilhain looked around for the source of Lornach's alarm. Immediately, he saw it. A vaporous fog had begun to rise from the stone floor of the battlement.

"Drùghoth!" Aranloth yelled.

Gilhain knew what they were. He had seen the sendings before, nearly been killed by them. But there was something different about them, now. Not only had they appeared this time in broad daylight, but the last had brought with them a chill that left ice everywhere. These brought with them heat, and though they seemed less distinct, less solid than the previous ones, they moved more quickly. And already they formed up into nine vague forms and swept toward him.

The eyes of the sendings burned with a white hot hatred, and in their hands they bore curved swords that glinted and sparkled like the water of a lake when the sun strikes it with slanting rays.

The forms of the Drùghoth were gray and wavery, and their approach was something like the shimmer of heat rising from a hot surface. As they drew near they gained more substance, and it seemed that sparks flew from their keen-edged blades, and their eyes had become like glowing embers.

There was stunned silence on the battlement. Gilhain drew his sword. He heard the same sound of steel slipping out of leather sheaths behind him. The Durlin were close, Lornach closest of them all. But it was Arell who found herself standing between him and those who had been sent to take his life. Arell the healer. Arell, who cured rather than killed.

5. A Dark Shadow

Brand felt a violent chill in the air, and a shadow obscured the already mist-dimmed sun. The chanting of the Halathrin continued, though he heard faltering notes within its rhythm.

And then, even as they reached a crescendo, the Halathrin abruptly ceased their ritual. Brand understood why. An elùgroth was come.

The sorcerer walked calmly around the narrow trail at the edge of the dark tarn. With him were elugs and hounds.

The world seemed to stand still, and into the dread silence the elùgroth spoke.

"A pretty little ceremony, for a nobody who is long dead."

Surprisingly, some of the Halathrin laughed. There was joy in the sound, their voices filled with a mirth that no human could match. For even as the immortals tasted of bitterness that men did not know, so also were they confident in their remembered joys.

Brand felt his heart lighten at the sound of their voices.

"Long dead, perhaps," Harlinlanloth answered. "Yet not a nobody. Halath did more than most to stymie the plans of your master. That is why you try to sleight him. And your hatred therefore speaks eloquently of his success."

"Yet I am still alive," the elùgroth said coolly, "and he is still dead."

"All things die," the girl replied. "Even Halathrin. Even *elùgroths*."

She said the last word with a venom that he had never heard before. He knew the speech of her people, yet nothing had prepared him for the emotion they could put into words. For them, words were power, they were the embodiment of thought. So he had learned, but to hear it was a different thing.

The elùgroth gave the impression of being less impressed.

"You will die now. All of you. Mortal and immortal, and the staff shall be mine."

The girl looked at him, still calm. "We are well matched, and these others," she pointed to Brand and Kareste, "are not without resources."

"I am Khamdar," the sorcerer said. "And I do not fear the threats of young girls, immortal or not. Even less do I fear the stuttering powers of mortals who reach out beyond their station and ability."

The great hounds spread out behind him, hulking things of tufted fur and muscle, eager to pounce at their master's word. Growls throbbed in their throats and the claws of their massive paws ripped the damp earth. Behind them the elugs, less keen perhaps, but still deadly in their way, took up positions.

Brand glanced at Kareste. He saw that exhaustion still hampered her, and something passed between them. She nodded. He would fight Khamdar and delay him, and while that happened she would destroy the staff. It was ready to be burned, and once a fire was lit it would take hold of the bier rapidly.

A moment later he saw her look at Harlinlanloth. There was a slight flicker in the eyes of the girl. The Halathrin understood and would be ready.

Brand saw also in Harlinlanloth's face the resolution that it must be so, else evil would always seek the staff, no matter how or where it was guarded.

Brand turned his gaze back to Khamdar. The sorcerer stood still, and yet he seemed to grow. As though a shadow fell over him, darkening and lengthening, he became taller, thicker, more massive. Nor did the growing cease. In a few moments he towered above them all, a gigantic form, clad in black, blocking out the mist-dimmed sun. Red fire, like flickering embers, ran and sparked along the length of his wych-wood staff.

The enemy had become massive, and Brand had no answer to that. But he attacked anyway, for that was who he was. He refused to let any obstacle, no matter how great, intimidate him.

The Halathrin blade earned long ago by one of his ancestors flashed. Khamdar, for all his size and power, seemed surprised. Brand took advantage of that and flung himself forward fiercely. Yet still the elùgroth had a chance to send a spurt of wicked flame from his staff.

Brand rolled and ducked. He came to his feet again, but the elùgroth had backed away. Now, the hounds and elugs raced forward. And yet Brand was not alone to face them all. Suddenly, the Halathrin were with him.

The immortals did not swell in size. Yet, in seeming defiance of the dark shadow that fell over them from the expanded elùgroth, the light that seemed to always shimmer about them shone brightly, and their pale swords glittered. They headed for the hounds and elugs, and Brand was free to keep driving at Khamdar.

The elùgroth backed farther away, but it was a feint. What he did next surprised Brand. There was a shimmer and disturbance in the air, and then Khamdar seemed to sprout wings. Great clouds of darkness billowed behind him, and he rose from the ground. With a giant leap his chill shadow passed above Brand and then landed behind him. Then the shadow moved toward Kareste.

Brand turned and raced after the elùgroth. Even as he ran he drew and flung a dagger, but it passed into the shadow with a sizzling sound. There was a scattering of red sparks, and then the blade fell smoking and broken to the ground.

Kareste had already set flame to the bier. She sensed the danger behind her and turned to face it. Instantly, she gestured with her hand and a wall of flame sprang up between her and the elùgroth.

Khamdar hesitated, but only for a moment. That was all that Brand needed. He was upon his enemy again, his sword flashing, and Khamdar spun around to face him.

The two of them fought. The massive elùgroth swung his staff in a mighty down-handed blow. Brand darted to the side. Fire erupted from the ground in a crimson plume where he had just stood, and the earth heaved and scattered rocks and dirt.

Brand stepped in, stabbing with the point of his sword. Khamdar deflected the blow with his staff, and then swung it around again. It whooshed over Brand's head, all shadow and streaking fire as he ducked, and then he moved in to attack again.

This time Brand led with Aranloth's staff. He did not swing it as a weapon; instead, silver-white flame sprang from its tip and he lunged forward with it.

Khamdar was ready. His own staff, gigantic as his swollen body, swept it to the side. The sudden jolt knocked the weapon from Brand's hand. Yet he summoned flame to the sword in his other hand instead and continued to drive forward.

Khamdar seemed shocked. There was doubt in the burning eyes that looked down as though from a great height, but still he sent a bolt of lightning sizzling through the air.

Brand dodged, feeling the heat of a hundred deaths pass him, and then the scream of a Halathrin from somewhere behind who had not seen it coming, or who had not moved as fast.

Brand glanced back. One of the immortals, charred beyond recognition, fell to the ground in a smoking heap of ash and bubbling metal from ornaments and blades. Brand knew he had made a mistake by looking behind him. He gritted his teeth and turned, but Khamdar had already used the momentary distraction to advantage.

The sorcerer had turned also and passed through the fading wall of flame that Kareste had raised. He knocked her aside as Brand watched, and she seemed too exhausted to even try to stand in his way. She fell into a crumpled heap.

Nothing now stood between Khamdar and the bier, and he reached for Shurilgar's staff that lay at the top of the burning heap of timber.

Brand, a sinking feeling in his stomach, leapt after him.

6. Relentless Swords

The Durlin leapt into the fray, but Arell was there before them. She ran at the sendings, crashing into them and causing them to stumble and slow. She paid for her bravery, for a spark-bright sword slashed through the air and struck her. What damage it did, Gilhain could not see. But smoke coiled up from the wound.

Arell was not done yet. In the midst of the attackers she drew a knife from her boot and stabbed. It sunk into the sorcerous flesh of the one who had struck her, but did no apparent harm.

The creature, too close to slash again, elbowed her out of the way, and though the blow would certainly have hurt, she recoiled as though with great pain, and wisps of smoke drifted from her clothing. Another sending struck at her, and she stumbled and fell, and even as she tumbled to the ground it delayed the enemy, for now they must trample over her body.

Arell had given the Durlin the little time they needed. They were gathered now around the king, and their swords met the spell-blades of the enemy. And though steel rang against steel, or its sorcery-created semblance, the weapons of the Durlin had little effect on the vaporish bodies of the attackers.

One sending broke through the ranks of the Durlin. It reached out with its blade, lurching toward the king. He deflected the strike, flicked back his own blade in a killing blow, but the thing still came at him.

Gilhain backed away. How could he fight something that steel could not kill? He spared a glance at Aranloth.

The lòhren was not that far away, but he was being attacked himself. Two of the creatures had spark-filled hands around his throat. Where their blades were, Gilhain did not know. Perhaps the lòhren had disarmed them, or maybe the hatred of the sorcerers who sent these things was so great that only the violent and slow death of their enemy would satisfy them.

There was a scream ahead of him, and a Durlin died. His white surcoat burned, and a flaming sword erupted with a spume of fiery blood from his back. A moment later another Durlin perished.

Gilhain stepped back further. He did not wish to retreat, yet he had no choice. He knew also that it was only delaying the inevitable.

And then Arell was among them again. Her clothes were rent by blade; blood-soaked ash stained the cloth around the tears, and pain showed on her face. What had happened to her knife, Gilhain did not know. How she was even alive, he knew less. Yet she was there, and in her hands was a bucket.

Gilhain sidestepped and dodged another thrust of a fiery blade lunging to kill him. He made no attempt to strike back. That was useless, and he endeavored now just to defend himself. He had thought that Arell would use the bucket as a weapon, but she did not.

The healer came up behind the sendings. And then she tossed water at them in a high arc. It fell down on them from above, splashing and sizzling as it struck the backs of the attackers. Steam rose in the air and unearthly cries of pain with it. But the attackers kept on coming.

Arell had done more though than get one bucket of water. She had gathered a half dozen soldiers and they each came behind her with their own buckets. These they had gathered from the back of the rampart where they were kept to help wash blood off the battlement floor.

The soldiers flung the water in their buckets at the same time. A wall of flashing water struck the sendings. Screams rose into the air and the spark-glittering swords dimmed and fluttered.

For once, the blades of the Durlin suddenly seemed to have more effect, and each strike caused pain and injury. The creatures screamed again, but then they gathered themselves and drove forward. Their swords burned once more, and the Durlin backed away.

"Water!" yelled Arell, and soldiers raced to retrieve it. But the buckets were further away now for the closest had already been used.

Time seemed to slow, and Gilhain knew that death hovered in the air all about him. There was a growing rumble, and then a crack of thunder. The sky darkened; a gust of air hit his face, and the sendings seemed a little less certain.

Gilhain spared another look at the lòhren. He was free of his attackers, and they seemed to shrink from him as he stood tall and spread his arms wide.

Thunder cracked again. There was a flash of light in the sky, and then the heavens opened. It rained. Nor was it just normal rain, but a downpour such as Gilhain had rarely seen.

In just a few moments water flowed in great rivulets across the stone floor. Massive drops smashed into Gilhain and the Durlin, wetting their clothes clean through. And the sendings hissed and smoked and writhed. The water was anathema to them, and their bright blades dimmed and then vanished, dissolved into the sorcerous air from which they had been summoned.

The sendings writhed and collapsed. In moments there was nothing left of them but a drift of steam and the faint echo of a faraway cry of pain. The elùgroths who sent them suffered for their demise, and a moan ran through the enemy camp.

Arell returned with the soldiers, but their buckets were no longer needed. They put them down where they stood. Water ran from their hair and dripped from their faces. But with a final rumble the sky lightened and the rain ceased. It did not peter out; it just stopped.

Gilhain looked farther along the battlement and saw, not really that far away, that it was still dry. Aranloth had called the rain, and it had fallen only where he had wanted it to.

They all stood there in silence, dripping wet, and the hot noon-day sun beat suddenly down upon them again.

Gilhain's gaze turned to the two dead Durlin, yet before he could even think of what to do or say Arell was already moving. There were others, and though not dead they were wounded, and she moved to help them. How she did it, how she stayed on her feet, he did not know, for she seemed just as wounded as they. There was blood on her in several places, and darkened rents on the cloth of her clothes where the swords of the enemy had cut her, yet she seemed to pay no heed to her own problems.

Gilhain tried to catch his breath. He was too old for this, and he felt his heart flutter strangely in his chest. At the same time, he felt lightheaded. Only Arell knew of these symptoms, for he had experienced them before, and she had given him a tonic to counter them. She had also said they would get worse over time, and he believed her.

He did not think his courage would ever give out, but his body would; she had warned him in her direct but caring manner of that, and he knew the time was not that far away. Closer, unless he could leave stress and toil behind for the twilight years of his life.

He thought as he rested. The relentless swords of the enemy would wear them all down in the end. He must do something, something different and unexpected to break the pattern that was destroying them. Only by doing the unpredictable, the completely unforeseeable, did he have a chance to upset the rhythm of the enemy. For no matter the setbacks they had, they always regrouped and attacked again. But the question was, the question that had haunted him for most of the siege, was what?

7. All the Days of Your Life

Brand leapt through the failing wall of flame. Beyond it was Khamdar, and the fire on the bier that had begun to rage.

The elùgroth was massive. He had become a giant, become more than any man could hope to fight. Yet Brand called forth the magic that was in him. A blue-white nimbus surrounded him, and it protected him from the flame.

But Khamdar was another matter. The sorcerer was a threat beyond Brand's capacity to deal with. And yet, even as he thought that, he caught the lie within it. Khamdar had increased his size, swollen into immensity. But it was illusion only, a deceit intended to cause fear and hopelessness.

And the thought that he was unable to fight him had been seeded by the sorcerer himself. Brand did not let that thought take root in his mind. He gritted his teeth, told himself that he was right, and even as he did so Khamdar shrank. He was become a man again, yet still one of the most dangerous men to ever walk the earth.

Khamdar must have sensed this change in Brand, for he hastened toward Shurilgar's staff. With a leap he was upon the bier and reaching into the flames for the talisman.

Brand was right behind him. Sorcerer or no, he could not stab him in the back. Perhaps Khamdar knew that, and so risked this moment of vulnerability. Instead, Brand dropped Aranloth's staff and reached out with his own hand, gripping the back cloak of his enemy, and the bony shoulder that lay beneath it.

A moment thus they struggled. And then Brand's hand reached around and clutched the elùgroth's throat. His grip was strong, trained since his youth in weaponry, and an iron will guided it.

The elùgroth turned, for he had no choice. And with a heave Brand pulled him away from the bier and sent him sprawling to the ground.

Brand swung around to face his opponent, putting himself between the elùgroth and his goal. The fire on the bier swelled and crackled behind him. The elùgroth rose from the dirt like a swaying snake, a creature that would not be pinned down in one place, a creature that no one could predict where it would go and what it would do next.

And like a snake the elùgroth prepared to strike. His face was contorted by inhuman rage, and wicked flame burned at the fingertips of his left hand, but just at that moment three Halathrin propelled themselves into him. They knocked him flying and went down with him in a mess of flame and tangled limbs.

Brand looked for Kareste. She was nearby. Three hounds were growling at her, their tufted fur risen in hackles, saliva dripping from their fangs. She held them at bay, lòhren-fire stuttering from her fingers. But the fire was dying and the hounds getting ready to leap.

Brand did not hesitate. He threw his sword at them. The Halathrin blade spun and wheeled in the air, silver light burning at its edge. It smashed into the beasts with a spray of fire, but he was no longer even looking at them. He had turned, leapt back, and grabbed Aranloth's staff from the ground.

There, for a moment, he hesitated. The elùgroth had thrown off the Halathrin and was ready to leap into the flames of the bier again to retrieve Shurilgar's staff. But at the same moment Brand saw one of the hounds, the great ruff of fur around its neck burning with a wreath of flame, crouch to leap at Kareste.

He did not know what to do, and had no time in which to make an impossible decision. But even as he hesitated there was a strange sound. It was a thrum, or a scream, or a mighty screech. It was like no sound that he had ever heard, and he felt it vibrate as much through his bones as he heard it with his ears.

From the bier rose a plume of black smoke, thick and turgid. Thunder cracked in the sky and the earth rumbled as though the very hills of Lòrenta had come alive and begun to march. A gale rose, slapping into Brand's face and bending the plume of smoke. Sparks flew in the wind: red, green and wickedly hot.

Above them, the dark plume bent further, reaching down toward them, and its shadow was cold with evil. Closer it came, and then a gust of wind howled and dispersed it.

"No!" screamed Khamdar. It seemed as though there was agony in his voice. The elùgroth reached out toward the bier, his fingers opening and closing, but the staff was gone, and the bier roared with flame so hot that he stumbled back from it.

The hounds howled. The elugs moaned. Khamdar fell to his knees. Almost, Brand felt sorry for him, for he did not like to see anyone or anything suffer.

"It is done," Kareste muttered. "For good or for ill."

Harlinlanloth spoke quietly, solemnly. "Thus passes the last symbol of Halath, he who died for his people. Now, only memory exists, but memory shall endure even through the long ages yet to come."

Brand looked around. The few hounds and elugs that were left alive scattered. Khamdar had lost control of them, but the elùgroth remained. Slowly, he stood.

Brand took a step toward him. But he was not alone. Kareste shuffled on weary legs near him, and the Halathrin gathered close.

Khamdar eyed them all. He made no move or threat. His wych-wood staff was gripped but loosely in his hand. And then he stretched forth his free arm, long and clothed in a ragged black sleeve, and spoke.

"You shall pay for this, Brand of the Duthenor. Listen and hear, for my words are truth."

The elùgroth's voice was cold and remote, and a strange expression had come over his face. Brand had seen something similar before on Aranloth, but only when the lòhren spoke with foresight.

"Everything you touch," Khamdar said, "will wither before you. Everything that you reach for, shall fall from your grip. All that you want will disappear. You shall not know joy, nor friendship, nor love."

Brand stood still, frozen in place. This was not foresight, it was a curse, and the elùgroth continued with relentless calm.

"Your luck will always run out. Ill-fortune will follow you. That which you do not want will come for you, that which you seek shall remain hidden. The great shadow of death will walk by your side all the days of your life, dogging your every step. You will never be free of it, and you will know that not even death, *least* of all death, will allow you to escape your woe. And yet you will die, for I will kill you. I will destroy you in fire and smoke, even as you destroyed the staff. And I shall tread over your ashes, driving them into the barren earth."

A great quiet settled over everything. It seemed that even the hills of Lòrenta listened to the curse, for there

43

was power in the elùgroth's voice to command the very stone that lay at their roots. And the dark tarn looked up at them all, motionless as an unblinking eye to bear witness.

Brand was shocked, shocked and surprised as he had never been before. For he had expected a fight, expected anything from the elùgroth, but he had not anticipated this.

Yet he would not cower. In response, he gave a nonchalant shrug.

"That's been my life already. Perhaps it's the life of all who live." Then he stood taller, and a hardness came into his eyes. "Your words mean nothing to me. But this sword," and he raised his Halathrin blade before him, "is something that I well trust. It's in my grip, and it will not fall. Nor will it disappear. Nor will it turn to ash and smoke. And soon you shall feel the truth of *my* words."

Brand stepped forward toward his enemy.

8. The World Shall Tremble

Gilhain felt the loss of the two Durlin who had died. Death had claimed many lately, but he had known those two, known them well, for he spent most of his time with those who guarded him, more so than even with his family. He sighed. Would there ever be an end to the dying?

The bodies of the two men rested now in the Durlin chapterhouse; two young men, hand-picked by Brand, loyal to death. And though they would be honored, though their families would be well looked after in times to come if Cardoroth somehow managed to survive, they were still dead. There would be no wives for them. No children and grandchildren. It was not just the men who had died, but their futures with them.

All over the city it was the same. Nearly every house was in mourning, for they had been touched by death. War was a waste; it was an unthinkable waste. And how many had been killed that otherwise would have become great poets, or sculptors, or healers or merchants? They were all gone, would all never be, and the ghosts of the future haunted Gilhain as much as the dread of the present.

He felt the sorrow of the Durlin who were around him. It filled the air and even the irrepressible Lornach was subdued. All their faces were grim, and they would be grimmer tonight when the funerals were held.

The evening was no time for a funeral, but there was no choice in things these days. The days were for the living to fight for their lives. The night was for funerals and dark dreams.

Gilhain straightened. He must not allow himself to become depressed. The whole city was watching him, and if he faltered they would follow; and the city would fall. He was sick of being attacked, of the enemy reaching out with the specific purpose of claiming his own life. He was sick of it, sick of it all, but he must play his part until the end.

Noon approached. The enemy massed again below, and it was clear that another attack was imminent. The men on the wall waited stoically. Everything they did lately was stoic, but they had little choice in that.

The soldiers stood quietly; the elug war drums thrummed away in their disconcerting beat. Gilhain was sick of them too, but he must bear things just the same as his men.

The dark ranks of the elugs chosen to attack marched to the front of the main host. They were a seething mass of enemies, fueled with a will to destroy and the sharp swords to bring their aim to fruition. Malice emanated from them, a darkness borne not just of hatred and the desire to kill and destroy, but also of foul sorcery whose depth was unplumbed and that knew no limit.

At that moment, with the defenders waiting in silent dread and the enemy poised to unleash the horror of war, there was a gust of wind. It touched the enemy first, moving among its ranks and troubling them, bringing their drums to a standstill. And then, with a light caress of the Cardurleth it lifted up banners and pennons, touched the faces of the men, and passed over into the city beyond.

Aranloth straightened. His eyes widened, and his hands formed white-knuckled fists.

"What is it?" Gilhain asked, whispering into the silence. "What new deviltry do you detect?"

The lòhren began to tremble. His eyes glittered, but as he seemed about to answer there was a crack of thunder.

A great boom rippled across the empty sky like the peal of a bell so vast that all the world would not contain its ringing. It seemed at once to reverberate through the battlement and to also come from the farthest ends of the earth.

At Gilhain's side Aurellin muttered. "There are no clouds."

Taingern and Lornach stepped closer to him, and Gilhain felt a shiver run up his spine.

They all looked around. The wind grew and hammered at them, beating at the white surcoats of the Durlin who surrounded the king.

Thunder boomed again. The wall trembled. Screams rose from the enemy camp, from its center where the tent of the elùgroths was pitched. The war drums started to beat again, wild and erratic, and then they died away into expectant silence once more. The elugs preparing to charge the Cardurleth milled around uncertainly.

The Durlin drew their weapons, but Aranloth glanced at them and spoke.

"Put them away!" he commanded. "Watch and see, and think of Brand, for just now, no matter the empty leagues that separate us all, he is thinking of us."

There was a third crack of thunder, louder even than the others. The very earth seemed to shudder. The enemy host fell to their knees and lifted their voices up to the heavens in a great moan.

The world seemed to stand still. And then a great plume of smoke, thick and black, filled with sparks and roiling power, rose above the enemy host. Like a vast tower, mighty as a mountain, it leaned toward the city as though to overshadow all Cardoroth, and then it was torn away in shreds and tatters by the gusty wind.

The enemy moaned and wailed. The darkness dispersed and the bright sun gleamed in the sky. As

47

though a great burden had somehow been lifted from his heart Gilhain looked around in wonder.

All about him men were smiling and breaking into laughter. They felt it too, whatever it was, though they understood it no more than he.

Aranloth stood tall. It was one of the few times that Gilhain had seen him smile, a smile free of care that seemed to make him look almost like a young man again. Tears ran down his clear-skinned cheeks, and Gilhain realized that the true Aranloth stood before him. Not Aranloth the lòhren, bearing a great burden and masking his thoughts from the world, but just Aranloth.

And yet he was still a lòhren. His white robes glimmered, and the power that was in him, always present but usually hidden, shone forth. That force was unveiled, and it wreathed him from head to toe.

Aranloth moved. Slowly, he raised high his arms. And then he spoke. His voice was resonant, and by the power that was in him his words carried over all the battlement, and Gilhain guessed even over all the city.

"Behold! Brand of the Duthenor, Brand the Durlindrath, Brand who left this city on a quest, fulfills it! At great risk, battling perils and temptations you cannot guess, he has struck a mighty blow at the enemy. He has destroyed a source of their power, a staff that aided them, that enhanced their strength and gave the elùgroths might. No more! So, remember Brand in your hearts, for he has just now saved your life. If he returns, honor him with great honor!"

There was a sudden silence, and then a ringing from the city. Bells tolled. Soldiers cheered. City folk threw their hats in the air and danced and laughed. Even the Durlin, eyes still alert for any threat, spared tight smiles for each other.

Gilhain felt his wife's hand in his own, and suddenly everything seemed right with the world. But that feeling could not last forever.

Within the hour, out of the disorganized mess of the enemy camp, strode three dark figures. They were tall, black clad, and angry.

They came before the Cardurleth. And when they spoke, the power that was within them carried their voices, for all three spoke as one, to everyone on the wall.

"This is not over, old man. Still we have the blades to bury you. Still we have the relentless swords of a numberless host to cut you down. We will *not* stop. We *will* prevail. That is as certain as day follows night, and then the night comes again. We will reduce this city to blood-stained rubble, and the world shall tremble at its fate."

As one the elùgroths ceased to speak. As one they turned and walked back toward their host.

Gilhain watched them go in silence, but Aurellin broke it.

"There was truth in those words."

Aranloth shrugged. The Durlin looked to their king.

Gilhain gazed out at the enemy. And then he also broke his silence.

"And there is truth in what I say now. We will prevail, for we have been given a chance beyond hope. Now, we shall turn defense into attack. Now, the hunted will become the hunters." He pointed out toward the dark host below. "The enemy shall learn to fear us. Too long we have stayed behind the great wall of Cardoroth. Now, Brand has given us an opportunity, and I will take it."

They all looked at him for a moment, different expressions on their faces. Most, he thought, were wondering if he were mad, if the pressure had finally unsettled his mind. He merely smiled at them, for a plan had come to him, a strategy that while of enormous risk could bring enormous benefits.

Aurellin, who knew him so well and knew that he had not lost his mind, narrowed her eyes at him.

"What are you planning?"

"Listen," Gilhain said. "This is what we'll do, and may fortune favor us."

9. More than You Seem

Khamdar stood there. The curse had left his lips, his black heart having given vent to the evil within it, but his arm remained stretched out, and the ragged sleeve that covered it hung like dead ribbons of flesh from a rotting corpse.

It did not matter. Brand advanced on him, and with him came all the others. A few moments the elùgroth studied them, his shadow-haunted eyes gleaming with hatred.

"This is not the end," he whispered.

Brand made no answer, but continued forward, his steps slow but confident.

Khamdar did not turn away to flee. By some art beyond Brand's comprehension he merely became more and more shadowy. In a few moments he was gone, nothing but a shadow flickering amid the fringe of trees marching up toward the hills, if even that.

"He is gone," Kareste said, and there was a great weariness in her voice.

Brand reached out with his thought. He found that the more he tried such things the easier they became. But he discovered no trace of his enemy. Yet he knew that they would meet again, at least once.

"What now?" Kareste asked.

Brand sheathed his sword. "For me, I must return to Cardoroth. The staff may be destroyed, but a massive host no doubt still besieges the city."

"I'll come with you," Kareste said without hesitation. "Though I don't see what help we can bring to them from without."

"We shall see," he answered. In truth, he did not know either, but he felt that that was where he should go.

The Halathrin were looking at him, those who still lived, and he bowed to them once more. They were a formal and ceremonious people, and they seemed to appreciate such things.

"Thank you," he said simply. "It was nice to meet the fair folk of legend." He would have said more, but Harlinlanloth had begun to smile, if sadly, at him.

She returned his bow with a curtsey, but the smile never left her face.

"So quick to see us off, Brand?"

"No, my lady, but you and your band have done all that you can do. I had thought that now you would return home and take news to your people of these events."

"I have already sent a messenger," she answered. "As for having done all that we can do, perhaps you're right. Then again, perhaps not."

"I didn't see anyone leave," Brand said with a frown.

She shrugged. "The Halathrin are skilled in such things. But it is of no matter. What does matter is this. We have a grudge against this Khamdar and his brethren, both for our people and also for ourselves. We will come with you, and what we can do – well, we shall see."

Brand bowed again. This was more than he expected.

There was little talk after that. They quickly prepared to leave, holding a ceremony for the dead and interring them in the earth. The bier still burned. Soon it would become coals and then nothing more than ash on the wind.

They left, and the fire dimmed behind them. Kareste led the way, for she knew Lòrenta and the surrounding lands better than everyone else. Brand followed her, brooding on his thoughts and problems. The Halathrin trailed behind, fanning out but moving in silence.

Kareste turned to him some while later. "I had not thought they would come," she said softly.

"Nor I," he answered. "But it's fitting."

"How so?"

"They've been wronged," he said, "and this is their chance to redress that."

"Revenge?" she asked. "I hadn't thought you the type."

"No. I'm not. But if you let people walk all over you, you only encourage them, and any others who see it to do the same. Sometimes you have to fight back – not because you want to, but because you must."

"It's a fine line."

"So it is, but you've just now walked on the right side of it. You destroyed the staff. It could've given you great power, and the capacity for revenge against the elugs who long ago wronged you and your family."

She looked away. "Perhaps," she replied at length. "But if I know where that line is, it's because you showed me." She paused again. "Truly, you're more than you seem. You know more than I think about many things, and you guess even more still. And you always have a few surprises up your sleeve. But I'm no longer surprised that Aranloth gave you his staff. Not in the least. And I think that now you have a greater appreciation of what it meant that he did so."

It was Brand's turn to look away. She had struck nearer to the truth than he would have liked, and it reminded him of his problems.

He was a warrior, perhaps one day a chieftain if he could free his people from their usurper. He wanted nothing else, especially not magic that he did not trust. But now a choice lay before him; to follow his heart's desire, or to accept a burden of responsibility and power that he did not seek, nor was wise enough to handle, and that in the end would see him weighed down with the cares of the world as was Aranloth. It was no way to live. But could he live with the knowledge that he refused to heed the call of the land, and the people who lived in it?

He did not answer Kareste, but he felt her eyes on him. She guessed much of what was going through his mind, and as he had left her free to make her choice, thus did she leave him to his. It was strange how quick, and how complete, the reversal of their situations had been. But fate was full of these little twists. Or if not fate, the chances of life.

But fate, or chance, or design did not matter. They never had to him before. He would forge his own path. At least, as soon as he knew what it should be.

10. Strife and Mayhem

Brand and his companions came down from the misty hills of Lòrenta. They were leaving that mysterious land behind them, and many strange things had happened there. Not Brand, nor Kareste, nor the Halathrin would ever be the same again.

An unusual feeling surfaced in his mind as he rode. Things had changed for him. Some for the better, some for the worse. But most related to the future, and he could not see where that led, for he had two paths before him and did not know which he should choose, if he even *had* a choice. And it was not in his nature to endure uncertainty or doubt. He must consider, and then decide on his action. Fate could go hang itself. But even as that thought crossed his mind so too came another: maybe for once in his life there was a power outside himself that was greater than his own will.

The Halathrin kept mostly to themselves. They were a strange people, quick and agile on their feet, keeping up with the pace of the horses. Brand had slowed down several times, but Harlinlanloth had only grinned at him and waved him imperiously on.

Brand did not quite know what to make of her. At times she seemed like any other young girl, but at other times she showed that she was a leader of people, and that she had an understanding of the world, born of years of living beyond his count, and a maturity that made him seem as a child. It was yet another strange feeling, and he sensed that she reveled in the fact that he did not understand her. In that respect, she was like most young girls that he knew: she enjoyed being a mystery but wanted him to solve it at the same time. Perhaps he would accomplish that. Perhaps he would not. Either way, he liked her.

The Halathrin travelled silently, almost invisibly, and Brand remembered that the famed Raithlin, the scouts of some of the Camar tribes in ancient days, had learned their arts from such as these.

"So," Kareste said, interrupting his thoughts. "What's your plan? Lead us to Cardoroth and get us killed?"

She had changed, but not in all ways. Her tongue could still be sharp. But that may have been because she knew he was thinking of the Halathrin girl. Kareste, for all her power, could also act like a young girl when the mood was on her, even if that was seldom.

"Hopefully not," he answered.

"Then what is it?"

"I don't know, but Cardoroth is where I must go. I'll think of something as we travel."

"Humpf!" Her tone was even more dismissive than usual, but he noted that she did not speak of going elsewhere.

Her question was nonetheless a good one, notwithstanding her ungraciousness. What aid could he bring the city, and his friends, now? But even as he considered that his earlier thoughts of the Raithlin came back to him. They were always few, but as scouts their job was to spy out the situation, report back on enemy movements, and at need sow strife and mayhem among the enemy. He was not a Raithlin, but with the Halathrin beside him, could they not kindle some sort of discord among their opponents?

It was a thought, it was the beginning of a plan, but it needed more work yet. Much more. He dared not even mention it to Kareste for she would tear it to pieces. And so she should. He must come up with something that she could *not* tear to pieces, no matter how much she tried. If he could do that, then maybe he was getting somewhere.

Eventually, they reached the Great North Road. It was empty and void of any sign of recent travel. Brand paused there a while to give the horses rest. He dismounted and Kareste followed suit. He chafed at the delay, but it was best to keep the horses fresh while they could, for it was impossible to say what hard riding might lie ahead.

One of the Halathrin approached. It was not Harlinlanloth, as usual, but a seemingly young man.

The warrior reached him, a slight frown on his face. His hair was that strange silver-white that seemed to predominate among his people; he had a slight scar that marred his face and his voice, when he spoke, though melodious in its way seemed rough compared to Harlinlanloth.

"The land here has changed little," he said casually. "I'm called Narinon, and I trod this road many times in my youth before the Camar came to dwell near our home in the south."

Brand, though he knew he should not have been, was somewhat shocked. This seemingly young man had been alive in a time that was no more than myth and legend to the people of Cardoroth. And there was an edge to his voice as well; it seemed that some of the Halathrin would not have destroyed the staff had the choice been theirs instead of Harlinlanloth's.

The warrior did not appear to require any reply to his comment. He carried on, almost, but not quite oblivious to Brand's surprise.

"Once, I even walked the mountains of the north, Auren Dennath as we call them. It was a fair land, and the memory of that lingers in my mind. Gladly I would walk there again."

"But the Halathrin no longer travel abroad," Brand said. "They stay in their forest realm and the land, and its people, miss them."

Brand knew it sounded like a compliment, but there was a rebuke hidden within it. The Halathrin no longer ventured beyond their borders to help fight elugs. They had not done so since the Elu-Haraken, what most just called the Shadowed Wars. Brand did not really blame them, for they had suffered much, but if this warrior resented the fact that the staff was destroyed to help protect the free peoples of Alithoras, he may as well know that resentment could be a two-edged sword.

The warrior made no sign that he took offence, yet Brand was sure that he understood exactly what had just been said.

"What are the mountains like?" Brand asked. Having delivered his rebuke, he wanted to change the subject; and talk of those mountains always stirred him for some reason.

"Dangerous," the warrior replied. "A small misstep there could be death, but that is so in many places of the world."

Brand did not answer, and the warrior went on. "There are ice flows and chasms and storms wild as anything you have ever seen. The wind howls among the peaks and the caves moan when the snow flies and the sky is dark. But those days are not the only ones. At other times the world is still. Nothing moves over snow so white that it nearly blinds the eye, and the pines, dark green and scented, march away over slope and ridge, through valley and dale, and a man could walk beneath their shadow all the days of his life, however long that be, and not walk the same trail twice."

Brand began to feel his blood stir. "And what of summer?"

The warrior laughed. "Summer is short, but the days are beautiful beyond your comprehension. The daytime sky is bluer than any gem of the earth, and at night the stars shine so bright that you feel that if you climbed a mountain you could reach up and pluck them all from the sky."

"And what of the elugs who dwell there?"

"Yes, there are elugs there, or there were. Rumor is that they still haunt the caves and dark valleys. They are one of the dangers, that is true. But they are not the only one. There are other dark creatures also, but the mountains are vast, and you can walk for day after day without seeing such as they, perhaps even weeks. And at those times, in certain places, and one in particular near the source of the river that flows down to fill Lake Alithorin, there is peace and tranquility such as even we Halathrin cherish, for it is found in few places on earth."

Brand did not like this man, but there was a certain passion in his voice when he spoke that was eloquent, a certain something in his words that found an answer in Brand's heart.

"Does this place have a name?"

"Of course. We call it Limloth, which in your tongue would be 'Still-peace,' or something similar."

"A fair sounding name."

"It's a fair place, fair beyond your imagining – even as Harlinlanloth is forever beyond your grasp. The one is likely too dangerous for you to reach, frail mortal that you are, and the other, the other is too bright for mortal eyes to endure. Her spirit is greater than yours even as the mountains rise above the plains. To try to get too close is to risk falling as from a great height."

Brand raised an eyebrow. There it was, the cause of this warrior's hostility. Now, he realized how things stood. But there was no time for this. Other things needed doing.

59

"I'll think on your words," he said coolly.

"That would be wise."

Brand looked at this warrior more closely. He was fair, pretty as a girl in many ways, but there was a steel in him, and a confidence too. This was a warrior who feared little, least of all expressing his opinions.

Time slowed. Brand looked him in the eye, and then he smiled. The warrior did not know what to make of that, but he did not withdraw his gaze.

There was a commotion behind them, and then one of the Halathrin stepped forward and pointed.

"Someone comes!" he said.

They all looked to where the man pointed. South, a long way away down the straight line of the Great North Road, a lone figure walked.

It was no wonder that the Halathrin had seen him first. They were reputed to have excellent sight, far better than an ordinary man's, and yet Brand could see the figure also.

Brand considered the situation. There was nowhere to hide for there were no trees here, and the land was flat and the grass not long. Besides, if they could see the figure, likely enough whoever it was had long since seen them: they were many and there were horses among them.

"What do you think?" Kareste asked. "If she had heard the warrior's words of warning to Brand she gave no sign.

"There's nowhere to hide," Brand said, "and perhaps no reason either. He's only one, be he friend or foe."

The warrior with the scar pursed his lips. "Few times is a stranger in a strange land a friend."

Brand leaned on Aranloth's staff. "I haven't found that to be the case, myself. But I'm not as old as you, nor as wise."

The warrior did not answer. However, Brand felt Harlinlanloth's gaze on him. Her expression was unreadable, but he knew by the very fact that she looked

60

at him, and then shifted her gaze to the warrior, that she guessed exactly what had passed between them. What she thought of it, he could not tell.

"Travelers are rare these days along the road," Kareste said, seemingly oblivious to what was going on. "It could be an elùgroth."

"Or it could be anybody," Brand replied. "We'll wait and see."

Kareste looked at him speculatively. "Trusting to luck, again?"

He gave her a wink, but did not answer. After a moment she looked away, the lòhren look of inscrutability on her face, and he knew that she also had heard or guessed what had passed between him and the warrior.

He watched the lone figure approach. He did not think it was an elùgroth, but there were others who sought Shurilgar's staff. Would they know it was destroyed? Probably those with enough power would sense that it was gone. But then, who was it that came toward them?

11. Now is Our Chance

They gathered around and listened as Gilhain spoke of his plan. He talked to them quietly, but nevertheless with excitement. And as he did so, he felt the anticipation of great events quicken his pulse.

"We've defended for a long time," he said. "Now, the enemy is in disarray. The staff is destroyed, the elùgroths are distraught, and the greatest sorcerer among them all is gone, drawn away from the attack by Brand." He paused, allowing his words to sink in. "What," he asked eventually, "does all that mean?"

"Trouble for Brand," Lornach said with a tight smile, and there was some laughter.

Even Gilhain saw the humor in that. The men around him, even as he did himself, used humor as a weapon against despair. And a potent weapon it was. Perhaps one of the strongest.

"And what else?" he asked, when the moment had passed.

Taingern spoke, quiet and thoughtful as always.

"The whole host is driven by the elùgroths. If they're in disarray, the enemy horde, mostly elugs, are in a worse state. It's the elùgroths who give them all purpose and direction."

Gilhain nodded slowly. He could not afford to move quickly here.

"And how can we take advantage of that?"

He waited patiently. He had deliberately not just explained his plan. It would be better to lead them to it, to understand the situation themselves and to make it their own.

Aranloth also remained silent. He, Gilhain was sure, knew exactly what the plan was going to be; at least the thrust of it, if not the details. And the fact that he remained quiet signified his agreement. If not, he would already have spoken. What he was doing, just as Gilhain himself must do, was time things well. The lòhren would speak at the right moment, and not before.

It was Lornach who answered Gilhain's question, and he was, as always, direct.

"You would send out a sortie to attack them?"

Taingern rubbed his chin.

"It's something we haven't had the chance to do before."

Gilhain looked from one of them to the other, but he did not answer.

"No," Aurellin said, adding her voice to the discussion as she always did, with quiet force. "I think he means a little more than a sortie."

The two men looked at their king, realization dawning on their faces, swiftly followed by surprise. Gilhain studied their reaction and liked what he saw; if he could surprise these two men he was a chance of surprising even the best leaders among the enemy host.

"Yes," he said. "I mean a bold attack." He allowed his voice to rise a little, allowed the passion that was in him to bubble up. A king could just give orders, but a good king did more than that: he motivated his men and inspired them.

One at a time, he looked both men directly in the eye and held their gaze.

"Now is our chance to do damage. Real damage. If we don't, they'll just regroup over a period of time and then start the process of wearing us down again."

"It's a great risk," Taingern said. "It might work, but it could fall apart as well. If they're not as disorganized as you think, then they'll counter attack. And we could lose many men, perhaps even have the gates taken by the enemy, and the end would then follow swiftly."

"That's true," Aranloth said. "Yet we all know that swift or slow, the end will come anyway. Unless we can do something *unexpected*. Gilhain has hit upon it there. Now is our chance, our only chance to strike, and I advise that we take it. We may lose our gamble, but we may win also. And if so, it would greatly even the odds. Without something else in our favor the enemy will do just as Gilhain says – wear us down."

Taingern, Gilhain knew, was naturally cautious. That's why he watched him the most closely. If he could win him over, he would have the others. Not that he needed to win anyone over. He could just command. Yet that was a slippery slope, and if people did not believe in what, and how, they were fighting, they did not drive themselves so hard.

Taingern continued to think his way through it. Gilhain glanced at Lornach. That one look was enough to see that he was all for it. After all, that was his way; he was an adventurer.

Then the two Durlin glanced at each other. They did not speak. Taingern could read the other man's face and intentions even better than Gilhain could. For all their differences, they were close. A moment Taingern held his friend's gaze, and then there was the slightest of nods. Few would even have noticed it, but Gilhain was watching. And it was what he had been waiting for.

"I've decided," he said. "We'll do it."

No one disagreed with him. They recognized that the decision was made, and they trusted his judgement. Especially when it coincided with their own.

Aranloth ran a hand through his hair. "A word of advice?" he asked.

"Always," Gilhain answered.

The lòhren pursed his lips and tugged at an earlobe. Evidently, he was still thinking his way through something and refining it.

12. Strange things are Abroad

They waited. And they waited quietly. No one showed discomfort or nerves, but they all must have felt those things. Brand did, and he did not think the others more courageous than he.

The figure drew closer. It was, after all, only one person, but nevertheless he relaxed a little as it neared and he could see that it was not an elùgroth.

There was a staff in the figure's hand, that much was clear. But there was no black cloak, no sense of menace. Whoever, or whatever it was, it was not a creature of evil.

They continued to wait. The figure came on, hastening down the road. It used the staff to help it walk, but it did not really need it. Brand was sure of that.

Soon, it was close, and Brand knew, with a sense of relief, that this was a friend rather than a foe. It was a lòhren, and there were few people that he would rather have met.

The lòhren was an old man. Frail even, or at least giving the appearance of it. He seemed older even than Aranloth, but was no doubt younger. Few, apart from the Halathrin, had seen as many seasons pass as the leader of the lòhrens. Yet regardless of seeming age or frailty, Brand never underestimated the strength of a lòhren, nor judged them for what they seemed. Aranloth had taught him that.

The old man shuffled near to them, and then stopped. For all his haste he did not appear out of breath. He gave Kareste a curious look, and then he bowed gracefully to the Halathrin.

"Well," he said in a matter of fact voice, "this is a surprise. Not a normal situation at all, with Halathrin and a lòhren just standing around on the road. What's going on?"

Brand considered him. He had said he was surprised, but in truth he did not look in the least bit startled. And though he recognized the Halathrin for what they were, and Kareste as a lòhren, he had said nothing about Brand himself. Perhaps that was mere random chance, nothing more than an expediency of time. But could it have been that he had omitted any comment because he did not know if Brand was a warrior or a lòhren? If so, Brand thought, he was not the only one.

Kareste took the lead and explained things to him. She did not hold back, for this man was a lòhren and she trusted him. Even so, Brand was a little surprised, for she said much and showed great respect.

Quickly, Kareste explained about Shurilgar's staff, how the Halathrin had been trapped by elùgai into the form of otherworldly beasts, and of their fight with Khamdar and the destruction of the staff.

The old man looked interested throughout, and he listened carefully, giving her his full attention. But he showed no surprise at anything.

"There is much news there, and some of it is new to me. I come from the south, the far south, and there is trouble brewing down there also. But that isn't all."

He leaned casually on his staff, but his eyes were intent as he continued to speak to them.

"Evil is abroad in the land. Beware! Not just elùgroths, but things darker and older. And they are vengeful."

For the first time since his arrival the old man looked directly at Brand.

"Now I know why. The staff drew them, woke them, but not all are yet dormant again. Beware! Strange things are abroad, and for some their hatred of you is personal."

"What things?" Brand asked.

"Just strange," the old man said enigmatically.

"Come with us to Cardoroth," Kareste said suddenly.

The old man thought about that. He seemed troubled, but that came across more in the time he hesitated to answer rather than in any facial expression.

"You might need my help," he answered. "Yet I have my own task. News of the south must reach the lòhrens. They'll need to hold council, perhaps then we can follow you, though you'll reach Cardoroth first. Some will come no matter what, that I promise. But at the end of the day Cardoroth will not stand or fall because of lòhrens. There are lòhrens and elùgroths enough there already. Its fate will be decided by other things."

The answer fell short of what Kareste obviously wanted, but she accepted the lòhren's decision with uncharacteristic meekness. Brand knew the old man could do nothing other than he had. Lòhrens were few in Alithoras, and the evils of the world many. They could not be everywhere at once. What could be done for Cardoroth they must do themselves, that and the soldiers of the city.

"Time is short," the old man said. "We'd better go our own ways."

The gave their farewells and parted, but the old man looked back over his shoulder at them and spoke to Kareste.

"Congratulations," he said.

"On what?"

"You passed your test. This I know – it's in your eyes. But we all pass such a test. Or fail…"

The old man walked away, but his words echoed in Brand's mind. They were said to Kareste, and yet the lòhren had glanced at him just as he had spoken. It was only a momentary flicker of his eyes, but Brand was sure of it.

The whole thing troubled him. How could the lòhren know that he faced a great choice himself, that he did not know how to proceed with his own future, and which task to take up?

Then he felt stupid. Of course, it could be more, but Aranloth's diadem and his staff were symbols, and not just a means to aid him. He should have known as much from the beginning. Symbols of exactly what, he was not so sure. But the old man had read the signs and understood them better than he.

"Who was he?" Brand asked Kareste.

"I don't really know."

Brand found that hard to believe, given how freely she had told him of what had been happening and what their purpose was. That doubt must have found a way to show on his face.

"Don't look at me that way. It's true. I don't even know his name, but I've seen him before. There are lòhrens … and then there are lòhrens."

She gave a shrug, and her face was thoughtful as she watched the old man hasten away into the distance.

"He may not have lived as long as Aranloth," she guessed, "but I bet he's wandered farther. Some of us travel, going from place to place among all the lands, everywhere but the far south where the elugs dwell. And *he* may even go there. That sort are healers and lovers of nature rather than advisors, as is Aranloth. But even they return from time to time to Lòrenta. They seldom stay long. You can also be sure that that old man has power, though I'm not sure if he ever uses it. Lòhrens are a strange breed." She glances at him sideways. "There's not really any one type…"

Brand pondered her words. What she said was true. But still, he had never heard of a warrior-lòhren, nor a chieftain-lòhren, nor a bodyguard-lòhren. He could only answer one call at a time.

13. Hilk Var Jernik

"An attack is good," Aranloth said. "But where should we strike? Some targets are better than others."

Gilhain knew instinctively that the lòhren had a specific target in mind, but he decided it was best to wait for him to reveal it.

"As Brand always says," Lornach offered, "Strike at the head of the snake. It's no good cutting the tail off bit by bit."

Aurellin flashed a grin at the Durlin. "You're a bold one, that's for sure. The elùgroths control the enemy, but they're secure in the midst of the host. We could pour the entire army of Cardoroth out the gates without hope of reaching them."

Lornach grinned back at her. "Maybe so, but if an army doesn't suffice, the few might accomplish what the many could not."

Gilhain knew the lòhren had something in mind, but he did not think it was this.

"No," the king said with some force. "I'll not throw lives away in some mad scheme to try to infiltrate the enemy by stealth. It can't be done."

Aranloth sighed. "It *is* a mad scheme, my king. But I would not go so far as to say it couldn't be done. In point of fact, it *has* been done before. Twice that I know of. Nevertheless, it's not what I recommend … at least not now, and not by us."

"Then what *do* you recommend?" Lornach asked.

Aranloth folded his arms across his chest. "You're right when you say that we must attack the head of the snake, but if that's beyond our reach, then what is next?"

They looked at him blankly. Gilhain thought he saw where the lòhren was going, but he was not sure so he remained silent.

Aranloth laughed. "Come now. If the head is beyond reach, then the next best thing is the heart. Where then is the beating heart of the enemy? What sets its rhythm? Come! The answer is simple enough. You've been hearing it now for a long time, and cursing it."

"The drums," Aurellin said.

"Yes," Aranloth answered. "The war drums of the elugs. They're sacred to them. They govern their life, awake or asleep, always beating. And they beat out the rhythm of destiny to that cruel folk. Destroy them, or damage them, stop them or slow them and the elugs will be reluctant to do anything."

"But how?" Lornach asked. "The drums are at the back of the enemy host, better protected even than the elùgroths themselves."

"Ah, Shorty," Aranloth said. "You're one of the best fighters I've ever seen, but you're not a strategist."

"No," Gilhain said. "But I am. And the answer is simply this – cavalry."

"Exactly," Aranloth said. "Cavalry. The war drums are sacred to the elugs. They're part of their rituals. Part of their life. They drive them on, and that's why they're at the back of the host. But cavalry can reach them. Riders could sweep out the gate, swing wide around the enemy, break through the picket lines and strike at the rear."

"Yes," Gilhain said. "Perhaps they could do just that, with luck and the right captain riding at their head, but returning would be harder. Much harder."

Aranloth nodded in agreement, but he did not say anything.

"It's a risky thing to attempt," Taingern said. "All the more so for the elùgroths will be aware of this weakness in their troops and will have taken precautions against such an attack."

Aranloth nodded, but again did not speak.

"No doubt there are precautions," Gilhain said. "But in all this time we haven't attempted such a thing. If we're quick, we can take them by surprise. Perhaps."

There seemed no real disagreement with the plan. Nor were any others offered. It was time to cast the dice, and Gilhain knew who he would risk such a plan with.

He gave orders to a nearby soldier, and the man scurried off in search of the person his message was for.

"So," Taingern said. "Which cavalry unit did you choose? And which captain did you send for?"

Gilhain glanced at Aranloth before he answered, and he saw that the lòhren was also interested in the response.

"None of the five." He said.

"But there *are* only five units," Taingern said with a frown.

"There are five *regular* units. Each a thousand riders strong, each with a well-respected captain. But for this mission, we need something different. We need someone bold, someone who knows that they may not come back, but who won't let that stop them. And better a few hundred of the most daring riders you've ever seen than a thousand ordinary horsemen. Speed will be their weapon here, not numbers. That is their only chance to get back in the gate when their job is done."

No one answered this. None of them knew there was a unit of irregular cavalry. Only Aranloth did, and judging by the serene look on the lòhren's face, he agreed with the decision.

It was not long before the captain came. Gilhain gave him his instructions privately, but he sensed the eyes of the others on this new man, assessing and judging him. And well they might, if they could, for this was no ordinary man.

Hilk Var Jernik looked him steadily in the eye while he was given his orders. He was one of the few men that Gilhain had to look up to when he spoke, and that was something that he was not used to.

The captain towered above six feet, and his shaved head with the long scalp lock trailing down his back made him seem taller. The jagged scar down one side of his face, and the heavy gold earring added to the picture of a man who did not blend in to any crowd.

He was certainly different from most men, not least in his expressionless face when told of the mission. Instantly, he understood the great dangers, and the great benefits if it could be accomplished, but he gave no sign of emotion at all.

Gilhain finished speaking. "One last thing," he said. "I'll not order any man, or those he leads, into such a dangerous mission. Will you do it?"

The man looked back at him. For the first time there was some emotion on his face, even the slightest of grins, as though he looked forward to this challenge.

"Of course, my king. I'll do it. It's what I'm here for, what my men are here for, exactly this kind of mission. But I'll offer them the same choice that you just offered me."

"Good man," Gilhain said. "And good luck."

They shook hands and then the man was gone, his long strides carrying him away with seeming eagerness.

When he was gone the others came over and discussed him.

"An unusual looking man," Lornach said.

"And not of the aristocracy, as the other cavalry captains all are," Taingern added.

"None of that is relevant," Gilhain said. "Tell me what you think of him as a man, as a leader of other men."

"He didn't inspire me with confidence," Taingern said. "He was too quiet, too withdrawn into himself. But a man may be like that and yet still be bold at need."

"And you, Lornach?"

"I feel the same as Taingern. But time will tell."

"Indeed it will," Gilhain answered. But there was a slight smile on his face, and when he turned to Aranloth there was a knowing look in the lòhren's eyes.

The sun was lowering, but much of the afternoon remained. The enemy host still showed no sign of attacking. The elugs at the forefront of the horde milled about nervously. Of the Lethrin, there was no sign. They remained hidden away somewhere in the host, licking their wounds from their previous humiliation. The elùgroths made no move. Their tent was dark and still. No one entered and no one left.

Hilk Var Jernik watched the enemy through the bars of the West Gate, the Arach Neben as the people of Cardoroth called it. He watched and waited while his men, three hundred of the best riders in Alithoras prepared. It was quiet in the city. It was quiet out among the enemy.

"It won't be long now, Jinks," his lieutenant said to him.

Jinks nodded quietly, and the man went back to oversee the preparations. Jinks, the men called him. It was a strange nickname, but he liked it. It was a play on his name, but more than that. It was a play on fate itself. For a jinx was something in the nature of bad luck, and yet they called him that in defiance. They knew he made his own luck, and they followed him without question.

They were all his extended family, he supposed. Mostly part of the same clan, and that explained their loyalty to some extent, but not completely.

What knit them together most tightly was that they were not of the Camar race, not even originally from Cardoroth at all. Their grandparents had migrated with other families from the west less than a hundred years ago.

The lands of his ancestors were grasslands, grasslands bordering a river. The stories went that they loved that country dearly, but pestilence had devastated them. Their numbers were too few to survive in the wild lands. And at that time the world was becoming a darker and more dangerous place. The stories went that elug attacks from the north had grown frequent, and there were too few warriors to stand against them forever. So, their numbers dwindling and their hope with it, they packed what they could carry and came east to the great city they had heard of, but had never seen and could not be sure really even existed.

But it *had* existed, and they had found a welcome there. And though they integrated, and learned a new language and took up the ways of the foreigners, still they kept their identity. They stuck together, and they kept the one great skill that they had mastered on the grasslands: horsemanship.

Some of them said that their tribe was distantly related to Brand's people. Some held that they were descended from the lost race of the Letharn. Jinks, for his part, thought they were a mixed breed, coming from both those roots and more beside. But it did not matter. They were his people, and he was their leader. He had earned the king's favor and risen to the rank of captain. It was no small feat for a man from a proud but poverty stricken people.

Jinks walked back a little way and mounted his horse. The three hundred riders were nearly ready behind him. The Black Corps they were called, and their mood was grim enough to match their name. He had told them what the plan was. He had told them they would probably die, but if they rode well, they may yet live. The trick would be surprise and speed. He smiled to himself. He had given them the freedom to reject the task, but they had not. Not one of them. He was proud of them, and by the end of the day all his people, all the poor and dispossessed, all those looked down upon by some of the native Camar; they would be proud of the Black Corps too.

He looked back and assessed the men. They were rough, just like him. Some were close relations, some distant; but he could trust them all. They were in this together. He knew each man, had recruited them himself, mostly from the poorest of his people. Many were criminals. He had given them a new home. He had fed them, put a roof over their head. In return, they had to work. Those who did not were ejected from the unit. Those who did – bonded. He saved them from a bad life, and they were loyal. To him and the others. They were as brothers.

He reviewed their weapons, measuring them up for the task ahead. The sabre they used was standard cavalry equipment. It was light, sharp and curved; ideal for the slashing attacks riders employed. Their stirrups were shorter than average, for the speed of the horse and maneuverability of the rider were critical factors that longer stirrups hindered.

The boots of the riders were of soft leather for comfort, but they also provided protection. The men wore no real armor; they relied on speed and they kept the weight of their equipment to a minimum, and the riders were also mostly small in stature, or at least very thin as was he.

But they had armor of sorts: stiffened leather greaves and jerkins. It was surprisingly resilient against sword strokes. Some wore caps of the same material, but Jinks did not think they helped much. Also, the legs and arms were the areas they were mostly struck at, being closer to reach for any attacker.

There were a few men who had the shaved head and scalp lock that he liked. These were mostly his close family. They held to the old ways of their ancestors longer, but it was a custom quickly growing out of favor.

Out of the three hundred one third carried a special bow. The black wood of its limbs was lacquered, and the weapon was small and lightweight, but nevertheless strong. Not as strong as a longbow, but still strong.

All of his men, archers or not, wore the standard black cloak pinned at the shoulder with a silver brooch. His fingers traced his own, feeling the outline of a galloping horse fashioned of jet. It was the only bit of jewelry that they wore, though some few others also sported the single gold earring that he did.

Jinks sighed. Another dying custom. And more than customs would die soon. Perhaps all of them were about to face death, and there would be fewer of his people left in Cardoroth. If the city survived, his people would disappear within a few more generations, absorbed into the great mass of the Camar race. It was inevitable, but there were worse fates than that. Cardoroth had welcomed and nurtured them. It was their home now, the same as for everybody else.

Drilk, his lieutenant, gave a sign, and Jinks knew the men were ready. There was nothing much to say now. They all knew what awaited them, and what needed saying he had said earlier.

"Good riding!" he wished them. They were the customary last words before an attack. "For the Black Corps, and for Cardoroth!" he added, which were not.

He held up his right arm, his light sabre gripped tightly. When it came down the soldiers who manned the gate would open it, and the riders behind would begin to gallop. There would be no fanfare here, no blowing of horns. There would be nothing to mark their venture, nothing to give away to the enemy even a second's notice of what was happening, nothing except the sound of steel shod hooves on cobbles.

But that was as it should be. The horses were what counted, for the men had a bond with them: the horses were the only thing that kept the men alive on the field of battle. And the men loved them.

Jinks dropped his arm. Slowly, the gate opened. The charge began, at first a trot and then a growing clatter of steel on cobbles until it rumbled as thunder in the vault of the tunnel.

Four abreast they rode, passing through the very same tunnel that their ancestors had used to enter the city long ago. Jinks thought they might be proud of the Black Corps if they could but see them now, riding to serve the city that had let them in.

In a grand column, the rush of wind and dark against their faces, they streamed out of the shadowy tunnel and came into the light. The road was heavily trodden and stained by blood. Elug bodies littered the way. The riders picked their way through the wrack of previous battles and the stench of death, and then wheeled gracefully from the road and onto what once had been green grass. It was now dust, the lush grass having been beaten down by countless elug boots.

Behind them many men filled the empty space they had left behind: foot soldiers left to close the gate and guard it against their return. He wondered how long the gate would be kept open. Gilhain would do so as long as possible. But if the enemy seized the gap between host and gate, the riders would be stuck outside the wall.

They charged ahead. The thunder grew to a deafening roar, and a cloud of dust rose slowly and hulked behind them.

The enemy was encamped to their right: unready perhaps, but like a living beast, massive and restless, and able to turn and respond. But how quickly?

Clear now of any obstacle, un-harassed as yet by any foe, the riders began to race in earnest.

A ring of sentries was thrown up around the whole city. It would not be hard to break through it and come at the enemy's rear. It was getting back that was going to be the problem, at least for those who survived.

The Black Corps could yet have a victory but suffer the ultimate personal defeat. But they were here for Cardoroth, not for themselves. And it was the result for the city that counted the most.

Jinks glanced back over his shoulder. His men were with him, and he knew it was in thought as well as deed.

14. A Great Honor

The days passed without event. Brand did not mind that. Each day saw him and Kareste ride, and the Halathrin spread out behind them, loping in their wake with an easy growing stride that ate up the miles.

The days were long and hard, and the nights watchful. Brand could not be sure what enemies were out there somewhere ahead, but few things in Alithoras were swift enough to pursue them.

They stayed on the road and headed north. It was dangerous to follow a beaten path, but the long sight of the Halathrin gave them an advantage; they would see an enemy before the enemy saw them.

About five days into their journey they neared the southern end of Lake Alithorin, and the dark forest that surrounded it.

There were indications that the road had been used: the old marks of the elug army that now laid siege to Cardoroth remained. And there were more recent tracks, mostly riders, but who they were and what their destination was, Brand did not know.

Somehow, the Halathrin kept up with them. Marching men could cover a surprising amount of ground in a day; not quite as much as a horse, but a lot. The Halathrin, it appeared, could do better. The fast pace of the horses did not seem to trouble them at all.

And when there was no danger, and when the way was clear all around them, the Halathrin sang as they walked. But sometimes they ran, and when they did so they moved with the gentle lope of a wolf, and Brand had a feeling that they could run all day and all night.

"They could beat us to Cardoroth, if they wanted to," he said one day to Kareste. "They can out pace a horse."

"So the legends say," she answered. "And they seem to be right. But what are they going to do when they get there?"

Brand shrugged. "That, I guess, we'll have to wait and see."

"Patience is a great virtue," she said a little tartly, "for those who have it."

That night they camped, as usual, well off the road. Brand built a small fire. The Halathrin returned to the camp after gathering some gnarled tubers, and these they roasted in the embers for a long time. When they were done, they let them cool and then distributed them. The tubers were quite starchy, but very sweet.

The night began to grow old. Many of the Halathrin wandered off, finding a place to sleep. Brand stayed near the dying flames, and Harlinlanloth came over to sit beside him. From where she sat on her blanket, wrapped up in her cloak a little way off, Kareste watched with dark eyes.

Harlinlanloth talked to him for some time, asking questions about Cardoroth and the king, and especially of Aranloth. Her eyes glanced often at the lòhren's staff that he carried, but she said nothing of that.

Their conversation was free and easy, and when she laughed it was like the peal of a golden bell and as though the sun shone at night.

She did not speak much of Halathar. Only that she liked trees, as most of her kind did. Trees, tall and green, thick trunked and ancient. She spoke of dim forest trails, and the task of her band, which was considered a reward for service.

"It's a high honor," she said. "We are each the best at something. I can sing, and chant, and work what you might call magic. One of the others is the best with bow and arrow, another can run faster than the wind."

Brand noticed that some of them had found time to construct bows and arrows – he was sure they did not have them before the journey began.

"Another is good at hunting," she continued. "And he," she pointed to one of her companions who seemed to be asleep, "can mimic animal noises and bird calls. Another can outswim fish."

It took Brand a while, but eventually he realized that this was not a random conversation. She was giving him knowledge of the band so that he would know what skills they had, and how best they might be used in any plan against the enemy.

"Lady," he said to her earnestly. "Why tell me all this? I don't command your band. I'm grateful that you've come – more grateful than I can say, but you're in charge of your own people."

She smiled at him sadly. "Always your kind and mine misunderstand each other. Truly, we're in your debt for what you did for us. That places us in your service. You command us, for the moment at least, until our errand either fails or succeeds. Not only that, you have the greater knowledge of the lands we travel and the enemy we shall soon face. You lead, and we shall follow."

Brand was surprised, and that rarely happened to him these days.

"But you're wiser than I. You're older, smarter, more experienced. Really, if anyone should lead, it's your place to do so."

She grinned at him suddenly. "Older? Yes, by far. But you need not be so blunt about pointing that out. As for wiser and more experienced, that has nothing to do with how old someone is. And you know it."

He was quite uncomfortable, but she looked at him sternly.

"You must learn to accept this, as you must learn to accept other things that lie beyond your power to change."

She smiled at him enigmatically, stood gracefully, and then left to rejoin her own people.

He looked over to Kareste who still watched him, her eyes unfathomable.

"Why me?" he asked.

"You know why," she answered. "You know exactly why."

He bit his lips. "I'm *not* a lòhren! I don't have the skill or knowledge or power to deal with different people, different lands, different races. I'm only a wild Duthenor. I've been told that often enough, and it's mostly true."

"That's not what I see when I look at you. Nor, it seems, what the Halathrin see. You are what you are. You will become who you will become. Accept it, as she advises, or run from it – if you can."

They did not speak after that. Soon, they laid out their cloaks and went to bed. It grew dark, for a cloud cover was beginning to build. As the night wore on, it became very gloomy.

Brand slept. Oblivion took him, and he had no memory of any dreams, pleasant or otherwise. When he woke, and he woke suddenly, it was some time before dawn, but not by much. Something had alarmed him, though he did not know what.

Everyone else remained asleep. The Halathrin kept watch; they had said that they needed less sleep than men. But they slept too. He saw only one that sat upright. He was atop an old tree stump, still as a stone, but then his head moved. His posture stiffened also. That he sensed something, the same something that had woken Brand was obvious. But what?

Brand took some deep breaths. Slowly, his hand reached out to the hilt of the sword that was always nearby, even when he slept. And then he waited, all his senses alert. He heard nothing. He saw nothing. Yet his heart began to pound in his chest.

15. Like a Spear

Jinks led his men at a gallop. The thunder of the horses rolled over the open lands surrounding the city. The enemy was massed to one side now, and they rode parallel to that. They were not within bowshot; neither within reach of the inferior long bows of the enemy nor within shooting range of their own black cavalry bows. Nevertheless, they were close enough to make out individual faces of elugs, and to see their surprise, even their fear.

But that great mass of the enemy to their right was not their target. Jinks changed direction once more when they reached its far edge. He struck out to the right, the horse he rode changing direction smoothly, the column behind him wheeling as one with his every move.

Four riders abreast was the column, and like a spear they hurtled toward the thin line that stretched out, vulture like, from the main host to surround the city with dark wings.

There was some attempt at resistance from the line, but then the elugs scattered like sparks in a gale. They had no bows. They had no pikes, nor did they even carry spears. Most of all, they did not have the training to stand before cavalry. Therefore, they did not have the courage to do so, for to hold firm in the face of a mounted charge took confidence and heart that few armies in Alithoras could muster. And that confidence came from training and practice, and finally from success in the field.

One elug, taller and fiercer than most, did loom up before Jinks. The creature held high its scimitar, preparing to make a slash, but at the last minute it panicked in the face of the rush of horsemen. Yet Jinks leaned forward, his own blade sweeping out and flicking across the elug's face. There was a spray of blood and a scream lost in the thunder of hooves, and then he was through. None fell beside him, and he did not think they would lose a single man breaking through the line, but this was not the hardest task that lay ahead, far from it. That was still to come.

Along the left flank of the enemy they now galloped. Some attempted to turn and face the riders, forming a shield-wall in defense. Jinks ignored their uncoordinated effort and rode on. This side of the enemy encampment, though ripe for an attack, was not their target.

A senior rider galloped beside him. The man smiled grimly. Another rode with the banner of the Black Corps unfurled on a staff. His lieutenant was some way back to reduce the chances of them both getting killed at the same time. But their mission here, though dangerous, was simple. Little leadership was needed.

The enemy host was massive. The column galloped what seemed a long time, and still the host hulked to their right. It seemed much bigger down here on the ground than it had from the wall.

Finally, they came to its rear and turned right again. The back of the army was a disorganized mess. There were wagons of food and supplies lined up in disorderly fashion and scarcely guarded. The enemy evidently had no fear of attack from Cardoroth, or from elsewhere in Alithoras. If there was time, Jinks would teach them that fear. But his primary job was to accomplish what the king had sent him to do: destroy the drums. And there they were! A long row of them.

The drums were large contraptions, covered in some thick, sun-bleached hide stretched taught over their wooden frames. Rusted iron rings hung from the sides, and long poles passed through them enabling four elug bearers to lift and carry them. And carry them they did, wherever the army went. A fifth elug served as the drummer.

Jinks veered toward them. As one his column of riders moved with him. There was a kind of channel between the supply wagons and the main host. Down this the column flowed like a river.

The drummers fled, but the pole-bearers held their ground and others came forward from the host to join them.

The hooves of the horses thundered. Jinks felt the blood of his body pound in his ears. The mad rush of battle was upon him, but not for nothing had he been made a captain. There was still a part of him that looked, analyzed and coolly considered. He had always been thus, and the greater the danger became the more this part of him came to the surface.

He saw at once that the elugs coming forward from the host were of a rarer breed. These were taller and stronger. They were better equipped too, drawing straight broadswords rather than the usual elug scimitar. The enemy was not as unprepared as they had looked. He must consider the possibility of a trap, but he was committed now, and trap or no trap, this attack was going to go ahead.

One thing, beyond any doubt, was to the advantage of the riders: the elugs did not carry spears. A defense could be made by warriors against cavalry, if they had courage, if they were battle-hardened and if they thrust a wall of spears before them. Without the spears, bravery was seldom enough.

Jinks led his men forward in their charge. The elugs held their ground, setting themselves for the clash about to come. The two forces drew close. Neither side flinched. Jinks took a deep breath. This was the moment; this was the moment that his people earned their place in Cardoroth. Or this was when his people died.

16. If Only I could See

Gilhain bit his lip. He did not normally show any emotion. As commander, it was his job, first and foremost, to be steady. Victory and defeat should not register on his face; that way men knew he was levelheaded, no matter the situation. That way he inspired confidence. He commanded first, and only allowed himself to feel emotion after his decisions were made. At least, that was what he strived for.

He stopped biting his lip. "If only I could *see*," he said with vehemence.

Aranloth turned to him. "Well, if you cannot see, then I shall tell you what's happening."

The lòhren turned away to look over the battlement again, an expression of intense concentration on his face as he peered over the seemingly endless ranks of the enemy.

They all looked at him strangely. "Surely," Gilhain said, "you can't see that far?"

Aranloth shrugged but did not break his gaze. "I can use lòhrengai to enhance my senses. It's no great thing, but it comes in handy. And Jinks, though you cannot see him, isn't really that far away. What I'm doing is only a slight stretch of natural sight."

Gilhain did not trust himself to answer. The lòhren made light of his powers, or else took them for granted as everyday things, but to others some of the things he could do were astounding. Perhaps that was one of the reasons he always shied away from revealing his abilities: it was yet one more thing that separated him from normal people.

The lòhren did not speak again for a little while, but when he did his voice, though low, held a thread of tension all the way through it.

"They ride," he said. "Even as I watch, they turn and drive toward the rear of the enemy. The elug war drums are there, as we knew they would be. But they are not undefended. The riders move well – I didn't know Cardoroth had such good cavalry. I trusted Jinks since first I met him, but he has done better even than I guessed. His men move with grace and precision."

"I've kept a close eye on him, and on his training," Gilhain said. "He commands a special troop. They are the best. The ordinary cavalry is drawn from Cardoroth's aristocracy, and they are more or less chosen by hereditary. Jinks is different. I let him choose his own men, scoundrels mostly, but I let him do as he pleases, because he gets results."

"They *are* good," Aranloth nearly whispered. "I see now a band suddenly breaking away from their column and riding ahead of the others. They gallop parallel to the elugs. Now, they draw their bows. Short arrows fly. A spray of shafts thickens the air. Incredible! The riders turn swiftly. It's marvelous to see. Back they come in the opposite direction and spray the enemy host again. What skill! They can shoot left and right handed, shifting their small bows as needed."

Gilhain nodded. "Jinks introduced that himself. He picks ambidextrous men, and as I recall, he was proud of the innovation when he told me of it."

"Now they turn again," Aranloth continued. "They ride very close this time. The arrows fly once more. Behind them the other riders take up a new formation. The arrows flit through the air, and the elugs fall, though the small cavalry bows aren't so powerful as to kill through armor, even just the hardened leather of the elugs. But many fall down anyway, wounded and bleeding."

Aranloth paused, watching intently, and everyone held their gazes fixed to his face.

"Now they wheel away leaving a gap," the lòhren went on. "The other riders surge forward. These have spears. They ride. They ride! Into the mass of the enemy they ride! There is a clash of flesh. Horses are down! Men have fallen with them. The elugs hack at the riders driving through their ranks, but the leather greaves on their shins help, and the speed and momentum of the horses helps more."

Aranloth gripped the edge of the battlement. His fingers were white where they clamped around the stone, but his voice remained steady, though not without emotion.

"Elugs screech and yell. The riders ride on. The pennons on some of their blood-wetted spears stream behind them. They voice no battle cry, but they slay in silence. Wait!"

Aranloth fell silent a moment. His face paled. "Jinks is killed! Hold! The press of the enemy is in the way. I cannot see clearly. No. He is down, but not yet dead. Three elugs pulled him from the saddle. Now they are joined by others and they try to kill him, but riders drive into the fray. Jinks is up again! Now he leaps once more on his horse's back and the riders all gallop on. He is at the rear of the column now. They wheel away!"

Gilhain watched his friend in silence. Almost the words of the lòhren drew a picture in his mind. He need not see the events unfolding far away to envision them.

"The archers come forth again," Aranloth said, "and more arrows spray. This time they are set with fire. Those men were not idle while their comrades clashed with the foe. Oiled rags flare, hissing through the strife-torn air. I have never seen that before, not so many at once so accurately fired. The arrows fly from up close. The drums are struck. They are pierced many times, both through their frames and the tight skin drawn over their tops. Flames catch. They have not got all of them, but many, very many."

Aranloth looked on grimly. He spoke slower now, his voice more measured.

"Yet more elugs rush forward. They try to put out the flames. The riders with spears come forth again. Jinks has planned for just such an event. The hard years of training show. They ride through and kill many. Among them now are some who cast their spears. But now they loosen water bags. I don't understand. Ah! They're not water bags but bags of oil. These they fling onto the burning drums and they burst. The skins must be very thin. And lo! Those drums they hit will not beat again!"

Aranloth laughed, and those around him grinned fiercely.

"Now they are off, all back in one column. They ride swiftly! Their work is done! Jinks leads them again. Now, they return."

"How many drums did they destroy?" Gilhain asked quickly.

"Thirty or forty. At least," Aranloth answered.

"And how many left?"

"Perhaps only ten," Aranloth said after a searching glance. "And some of those are damaged as well."

"It's as much as we could hope for. Perhaps even better than we could ever have hoped for. But how many elugs were slain?"

"Hundreds," came the sure reply of the lòhren.

"That's not really that many, but it never was going to be. This was about the drums, and uncertainty. We *have* taught the enemy that they're not safe. No matter where they are. None are safe."

"That is so," Aranloth said. "But it's not over yet. It's not over by far."

"Yes. They still have to make it back."

"No," Aranloth answered. "That's not what I mean."

17. All Dead Men, Now

Jinks kept riding. He was tired, and his horse more so. Not only that, there was a gash in its left foreleg. It bled profusely, but at least so far, it was not greatly hindering his mount's speed.

The column needed to hasten back toward the gate if it was any chance of making it home: but before him Jinks saw opportunity.

His riders had achieved their goal with the drums. It would have an impact on the elugs, much more a mental one than a physical, for they believed in a range of superstitious nonsense. But nonsense or otherwise, what mattered was that they believed it. Therefore, the destruction of their drums would hinder them. But now, beyond hope or expectation, was an opportunity to inflict real and physical damage.

They had not known when they planned the sortie that there were supply wagons here, so close to the drums. The king knew more about elug armies than most, and Aranloth more even than he. They would have talked the situation over before they summoned him, but if they had known the location of the wagons, they had said nothing, calculating the risks of finding and attacking them too high.

And there *was* great risk. Already the enemy would be moving to cut off their retreat back into the city. At least they would be if they were half competent, and a captain who assumed that his opponent was incompetent was the kind of captain who never lived to lead his men for long.

Jinks rode on, the mass of the enemy to his left, the wagon trains to his right. He was undecided, but not for long. It was for such decisions that he had been given command. He had freedom of choice here; the king encouraged that in his leaders. He wanted them to show initiative, to be bold when required, and to be cautious also, when that was needful.

Cardoroth remained badly outnumbered. The outlook was grim. Now, if ever, was the time to be bold. And so Jinks made his choice.

He gave a signal to one of the men who rode near him. This rider withdrew a small horn and blew a shrill note. The column of riders knew what that meant, must have guessed themselves that it was coming. They would have seen the same opportunity that he saw, would have just as quickly calculated the risks. But they did not hesitate.

The archers peeled away from the main column. They unleashed a hail of arrows, killing many of the scattered guards who stood before the wagons. The other riders came in, engaging the remainder with sword and spear. While this happened, the archers rode among the wagons.

There were no fire arrows left, but there was oil. This they cast over as many wagons as they could. Jinks had a quick look inside some, and he saw that they were stacked with sacks of grain and dried meat.

The wagons were close together. Jinks, for all his worry of underestimating the enemy, shook his head. Foolishness. There were hundreds of wagons, all in close proximity. His men could not burn them all, but they could get some, perhaps as much as a quarter if they were very lucky. And fire spread in such conditions.

In now they all went, riding slow, skirmishing here and there as necessary. Many dropped down on foot, for the wagons were too close to ride between. There they set fire to their wooden bases and canvas tops. Up the wagons went in flames, and black smoke roiled into the heavens. Jinks had never seen anything so grim and so pretty at the same time.

Out now from the host charged thousands of elugs. An elùgroth came with them. Jinks gave a signal and the archers galloped forth to meet them. It was token resistance, for so few against so many could not prevail, even mounted warriors against infantry. But it would slow down the charge and allow time for just a little bit more damage to be done to the wagons.

More went up in flame. Waves of heat beat at the riders, and a great roar and crackling filled the air. Jinks knew it was time to withdraw. It was now or never. They were already in trouble. Too long they had delayed, but the chance to wreak such havoc was worth it. They were all likely dead men, now. But they would *try* to return.

Jinks thought quickly. They could flee, yet to where? The enemy possessed cavalry. They were not as good, but Hvargil's force was a thousand strong. They would hunt the Black Corps down if they fled, for they could not allow such an attack to go unpunished. Nor could they allow such a force freedom to launch further assaults from the wilderness. It was better to fight now, to wreak more damage on the enemy and try to make it back to the city.

They swept out and away from the wagons to rejoin the archers. But even as they did so flame spurted from the elùgroth's wych-wood staff.

Men went down. Horses screamed. Jinks signaled again and the man nearest him blew his horn. The riders gathered together, forming a column again, and they wheeled and shot away in one formation.

Yet there was more fire; fire that leapt and bridged the gap, fire that hit one man and sizzled before jumping like lightening to another.

More men died. More lives were lost. Lives that might have been saved had they fled earlier. But Jinks knew in his heart that he had made the right decision: not for his men, but for Cardoroth. And his men knew that too.

18. Something Stirs

The Halathrin warrior atop the tree stump looked straight at Brand. Somehow, the immortal knew he was awake, though he had barely moved.

The warrior gave a warning gesture, but he made no other move except to slowly turn his head back and forth to scan the darkness.

Brand woke Kareste. All it took was a light touch to her shoulder and her eyes flicked open.

"What is it?" She whispered.

"I don't know. Something. Something out in the dark. Wake the others."

She did not ask any questions, but straightaway slipped from her make-shift bed.

Brand, crouching low so that he was not silhouetted against the horizon, made his way to the Halathrin guard atop the tree stump. The warrior was tall and thin. His face seemed chiseled out of marble, and his eyes gleamed in the dark. There was very little light, for the cloud cover was heavy, but it was near dawn and the first traces of the rising sun grayed the eastern sky.

Even in the dim light Brand could make out the alert look on the immortal's face.

"What is it?" he asked softly.

The Halathrin did not stop looking out into the dark, but he shook his head slowly.

"I don't know."

Brand waited beside him, silent and still. After a few minutes a light drizzle began. There was a pitter-patter of drops on the grass. The tops of the trees swayed at the touch of a slight breeze, and the air bit with a momentary chill.

Toward the center of the camp the near-dead embers of last night's fire began to smoke, hissing faintly at the touch of the water drops.

The others were all awake now, waiting and still, prepared for something to happen. But prepared for what?

In the distance a nudaluk bird called, knowing that dawn was at hand. A great flock of night-flying ducks passed overhead, their wings beating the dark air and their calls loud as they sought out nearby wetlands.

And then there were eyes in the dark. Some sort of beasts wandered around. Brand could not see them properly, but likely enough they were creatures of the elùgroth.

Khamdar was near, very near, but there was no sign of him. Nor did the beasts attack.

"What are they waiting for?" Brand whispered to the Halathrin.

"I don't know."

The drizzle grew heavier. Smoke was now thick in the air, for the rising breeze had stirred the old fire to life. There was no point in putting it out though. The enemy knew where they were.

Then out of the silence there came a sudden but muffled noise. Brand looked toward the camp. Two of the Halathrin were down. They thrashed on the ground, their faces blue even in the pre-dawn light. But no enemy was there.

Brand did not know what to do. Should he go back to help? Should he keep his eyes on the dark perimeter whence any attack must come?

He ran back into the camp. The Halathrin still thrashed, but their movements were growing weak. He saw that their necks were broken, and a sickening feeling overcame him. How could that have happened? There was no enemy in the camp?

As he stood there looking around wildly, Harlinlanloth came up to him. She seemed cool and resolute, but he sensed her feelings beneath that mask: the death of her companions was painful to her on levels beyond what a mortal could understand.

"Elùgai," she said definitively.

Brand cursed himself for a fool. Of course it was elùgai, of course it was Khamdar. And yet the sorcerer was not in their camp, and the beasts still did not attack.

Smoke roiled all around now, thick, swirling, turning and twisting under the influence of the breeze that had brought the drizzle.

A moment longer he stood there, undecided and uncertain, and then a realization hit him.

"The smoke!" he yelled. "The sorcery is in the smoke!"

He knew it was true, and even as he spoke the vaporous air grew suddenly hard. It was not yet around his throat, but he felt it creeping up his body like a disembodied arm seeking to strangle him.

Kareste was suddenly there. "The fire!" she yelled. "Put it out!"

But the smoke was everywhere now: tearing, twisting and tightening. And in the midst of the old fire's embers, something stirred. Sparks flew. A column of flame rose from the ashes, writhing in the dark air. An image was in it, and it was the semblance of Khamdar.

Sparks shot from the sorcerer's eyes, and they streamed from his hair. His arms were upraised. Strands of smoke, twining like rope, came from all his fingers. The camp shimmered with heat. The people were obscured by swirling smoke. A noise came to Brand's ears, and it was the hissing of rain and steam in the air, but to him it sounded like laughter. And then the grinning image of Khamdar looked straight at him.

19. They Will Tell their Children

Jinks rode at the head of the column again. They had flanked the enemy host once more, and now the army was to their left. But ahead of them was the picket line that spread out around the city.

They raced ahead. The elugs in the line scattered, not even making an attempt to stop them. In a few moments all the riders were through.

"That was easy!" the man near him said, a fierce grin on his face.

Jinks thought so too. But the knowledge did not give him the momentary pleasure it gave his companion. It had been *too* easy. The elugs had not tried to hinder them, and that meant, likely enough, that they knew a greater hindrance was already prepared. No need to risk death when the true confrontation lay ahead.

And so it proved. Though he was ready for it, Jinks still felt his heart sink when they wheeled around the host again and turned left, left toward the Arach Neben and the safety of the city. But there was no safety to be found there.

What they had all feared had come to pass. The enemy had launched an attack against the gate. The soldiers of Cardoroth had come forward. Some of the best troops were there, and they fought with skill and ferocity. They would hold the gate open as long as possible, but skill and courage were not a match for far greater numbers.

And the elugs swarmed against the soldiers in seething multitudes. Slowly, surely, the men of Cardoroth were being driven back.

There was one last resort for Jinks to try. There were other gates into the city, and though the picket lines before them were strengthened in those places, just maybe they had not come forward to bar entry. Just maybe.

But then he heard the thunder of hooves, and it was a noise that was not from his own men. It was from farther away.

Hvargil's cavalry had come forth at last. Some came from the right, blocking the way back from where Jinks had just come. Others now appeared from the left, blocking that way too. The Black Corps was trapped, and every member of the regiment knew it. The column faltered, and many of the men cursed loudly.

Jinks slowed to a trot and his lieutenant hastened forward to speak to him.

"There's no escape from this," the man said.

"It would seem not," Jinks answered regretfully.

"None of the men will blame you, sir. We will surely die now, but it was worth it for damage to the supplies. A hungry army doesn't fight for long."

Jinks knew that this was true. His men had struck a great blow against the enemy, a blow when they were already of low morale. He had done more than could have been expected of him, and he had given the city he loved a greater chance of survival. But there were probably already other supply wagons coming up from the south. The wound his men had inflicted would, sooner or later, be healed by the enemy. Still, in the meantime, it might provoke an act of rashness that Gilhain could turn against them.

Jinks gave a signal. Without hesitation the column moved smoothly. They trotted now, forming a circle, their movements precise and even. Jinks, ringed by all his men, able to address them all now at the same time, spoke loudly.

"We will fight!" he said. "There's nothing left for it. We will fight, and we will take as many of the enemy with us as we can. And away in Cardoroth, the lords and the ladies, and those who looked down on us in our former lives, they shall know pride! They will tell their children, and their grandchildren that they knew us! The riders of Cardoroth. The Black Corps!"

The company gave a mighty cheer, and then they came smoothly out of the circle and formed a column again. Like a well-cast spear they drove forth, but not at the approaching cavalry to either side; instead Jinks led them directly toward the rear of the enemy attacking the gate. This would make it easier for the soldiers of Cardoroth to retreat and secure the Arach Neben behind them.

The Black Corps struck with precision, unleashing a hail of arrows and then smashing into the poorly defended rear of the enemy. There was great slaughter, and the elugs fell by the score. As the riders drove deep into the enemy ranks they heard from afar the sound of battle on the other side of the attackers, from the battle being fought near the gate.

Jinks gave another signal and the archers of the Black Corps broke away, half to the left and half to the right. They fired arrows, keeping the enemy riders away briefly, but their supply of shafts was growing thin. Their victory with the wagons was coming back to haunt them.

Hvargil's cavalry did not have their own archers to return the attack. Their charge faltered, but they regrouped and when they came again there were too few arrows to halt their charge.

The enemy now came at the Black Corps from three sides, surrounding them, for the rear of the elugs had also stiffened their resolve.

Jinks fought with his sabre, as now did all his companions. They were ringed around, pressed close, and the advantage of their mounts was reduced. Swiftly they began to fall in the face of such an onslaught and of the three hundred there were perhaps now only fifty men left alive. They were close now, all together for their last stand. Jinks was still there among them, his sabre broken and lying on the field but an elug scimitar in his steady grip instead.

The enemy riders closed in. The elugs at the gate were better prepared now, and they had turned a flank to them and commenced to advance, swords crashing against shields in a mighty tumult meant to intimidate.

Jinks glanced skyward, offering a momentary plea to the universe; but he knew no such appeal would be answered. The clouds hanging low overhead were dark. In an abstract way he noted that rain was on the way. Or perhaps even a storm. He squinted. Yes, definitely a storm. He could feel it build, and a gust of wind tossed his scalp lock.

All his men were steady about him. They knew what came next; it took no genius to contemplate that. He looked about him with a certain pride.

"One day is as good as another to die," he said.

Somewhere a horse snorted and stamped a hoof. Some of the men gave nods of agreement at their leader's words. Jinks worked his way to their front, getting ready to face the advancing elugs.

"One more charge at the enemy!" he shouted. "It will be our last, as well you know, but long will Cardoroth remember it!"

He gathered his reins tightly into his trembling hands, and was about to nudge his horse into a gallop. But at that moment a flash of lightning streaked across the darkening sky. Thunder pealed like the crack of doom and then rumbled away into the distance.

Jinks looked up at the Cardurleth, behind which lay all that he loved. Yet upon the battlement he saw Aranloth. And with him were now gathered other lòhrens. They had come to join their leader from their usual places along the wall, and they now stood in one group behind him.

Aranloth held his arms high. A white light was about him. Jinks looked, and he paused as he watched, the reins forgotten in his hands.

All about him leaves and dust and grass stems swirled in the air. The wind whipped into his face. Lightning once again cracked. This time it struck in the midst of the elugs before the gate. Jinks looked at the enemy. He heard their screams. He felt their panic. And he sensed their primal fear.

Again and again the lightning tore apart the sky and stabbed, dagger like, into the middle of the elug ranks. The smell of smoke hung heavy in the air. There were more screams, and at last the panic grew so great that the elugs fled. They scattered left and right, for there was no lightning to either side. A gap opened. Jinks saw, as though through a widening tunnel, the soldiers of Cardoroth before the gate.

Yet though he saw a chance of life, a chance to enter the city that he could not have hoped for, straightaway it was dashed. No man would dare such a storm, for now the lightning struck ever more swiftly, and a vortex of dust and debris spun where the elugs had but recently blocked the way. No man had the courage to risk that road, no matter what lay at its end.

Jinks shuddered, and then looked up at Aranloth. The lòhren in his turn looked down upon him. From all that distance Jinks sensed his gaze, and then something more. Dimly, as though from very far away, he heard the lòhren's voice. And it was filled with urgency.

"Ride! Ride to the gate! Fear no storm! Fear no lightning. Ride! Ride and live!"

Jinks looked at his men. A moment thus he hesitated, and then he acted.

"We ride!" he called. "The storm is our friend. Ride now and live!" His command echoed the lòhren's words.

Those of the Black Copse who yet lived looked at him in disbelief, but when he kicked his own horse forward they followed.

The riders gathered speed. Lightning hissed in the air all around them. It sizzled and boomed. And yet ... and yet Jinks noticed that no scorch marks showed on the ground. Nor had any fires started amid the dry and trampled grass. Most of all, there were no dead bodies of elugs. Where the army had stood, the field was empty of stricken corpses as surely there should have been.

"It's illusion!" he yelled to his men. On he rode, and his men rode in a tight group behind him. The vortex of air spun upward and disappeared. The soldiers before the gate retreated back into Cardoroth.

Jinks rode onward. Now there were dead bodies, but these elugs had been killed by steel and not lightning. Their wounds were proof of that.

And then beyond any hope that he had foreseen, Jinks led his men into the tunnel of the Arach Neben. It was dark. Behind him he heard the clang of the great gate as it shut.

Soldiers were now all around, helping him and his riders down. They began to tend the wounded and they led away exhausted mounts. This was not easy, for some of the horses had become terrified and they pranced and shied and only the soft and repeated words of their riders brought any semblance of calm.

Jinks looked around. He saw that less than fifty of the three hundred had made it back alive. But the enemy had suffered a major defeat.

It was worth it. And his men had absolved themselves of guilt; the pickpockets, the confidence men, the burglars and the tricksters. That was worth it too, for guilt was worse than death, and his men, every one of them, knew it. And he knew it too, and even as his legs gave out beneath him he exulted, for his people had become a legend that would endure so long as Cardoroth stood.

20. Tall and Terrible

Khamdar, or at least the image of him that hung in the smoke, grinned. Fire curled from his mouth. His hair streamed rivers of fire.

The sorcery of the elùgroth was great. They all seemed trapped by his power. Some were pinned to the earth by smoke become substance. Some were being choked. Brand was thrown back to sprawl helpless on the ground.

He lay there, half stupefied by the force that had hurled him away, but his mind still asked questions and groped for answers. Why had he been hurled away? Slowly, the answer came to him: to keep him away from the fire.

Slowly but surely, he began to stand. It took all his strength. The smoke tried to pin him down and then, like a seeking hand, it reached for his throat.

Nevertheless, he pushed forward. Having come to his feet he stepped, and his steps, though each one seemed like climbing a mountain, were inexorable.

The force thrown against him redoubled, but he pushed forward anyway. He had a grudge against Khamdar. The sorcerer had dogged his steps for a long time now. Khamdar had killed many innocent people. The conflict between them had become a contest of will against will, and that was what really lay behind the struggle. The smoke was little more than illusion.

Sweat broke out all over Brand. He was dripping wet by the time he neared the fire and gasping for breath.

Khamdar rose in a plume before him, tall and terrible. Brand ignored the image. He knew that his blade could not hurt such a phantom. Instead, he deliberately struck into the fire itself and scattered embers wide and far.

Again and again he struck, and then he was kicking as well. The fire flared brightly. He felt the heat of it, and then it was gone. Khamdar simply evaporated. Smoke clogged the air, but now, though thick, it was nothing more than a reeking cloud that drifted without intent.

Brand looked around. Some of the Halathrin were dead. This was yet another crime added to Khamdar's long tally. One day, Brand knew with sudden certainty, there would be a reckoning. Khamdar would be held to account, or Brand himself would die. There was no doubt in his mind that that time would come, and he had a feeling it would be one day soon. Brand knew that he did not have the sorcerer's skill, perhaps not his power, but nevertheless that day of reckoning would come, and the elùgroth would know fear as he had never known it before. Silently, Brand swore it.

The living Halathrin looked bleak. Harlinlanloth, grim as the others, looked determined also.

"We will make him pay for that," she said, as though she had read his thoughts. "It is one more evil against us, one more call for justice that will one day be answered."

He realized that she had not perceived his thoughts at all. It was just that she felt about the sorcerer exactly as did he.

"You and I both," he answered. "I have my grudges, and you have yours. He shall not escape us."

Kareste shook her head. "Dreaming of revenge against such as he is sweet, but that's all it is – dreaming. Khamdar is greater than us, and he nearly beat us all though he was but now a phantom. The real him is miles away. If you would oppose him, bear that in mind. Fear him, and fear him greatly. Fear him, and you might yet live. Fear him the

111

more so, for our band grows weaker after every encounter."

Brand cocked his head. "You're right, and yet why did he send a phantom against us? Perhaps he is scared even as are we?"

None of them had any answer to that, and soon they moved on to the ceremony for the funeral of the fallen Halathrin. This was not so elaborate as the earlier one, yet still it had that somber feel to it, that sense of otherworldliness that the Halathrin brought to everything they did.

Without making it obvious, Brand studied Harlinlanloth. She showed little overt emotion, and yet he saw the deep sorrow in her eyes. Nobody understood death, and the immortals, who experienced it so rarely, must understand it less.

When she was done she walked past Brand, and her momentary glance stabbed him to the heart. She was hurting, and there was nothing he could do to take the pain away. It was one more mark against Khamdar, one more crime for which Brand would hold him to account – if he could.

They struck out to the east and toward Cardoroth. Ever they watched for Khamdar, or for some trap that he had left for them to spring, some ambush of beasts or men or elugs. But they saw nothing. Nothing at least until the Halathrin pointed out to Brand the tracks of the elùgroth.

Khamdar, like all elùgroths, wore boots. And a design was worked into their soles: a drùgluck sign. Brand had heard something of it before, but the Halathrin warrior traced the marks with his fingers and then spoke to him quietly.

"The mark of ill-omen. He wants us to see it. It is a warning."

They went on, and sure enough the marks became much plainer. Khamdar had made no attempt to hide his passing, even at times going out of his way to deliberately stand in damp earth to leave a trail. Evidently, the drùgluck was a warning, but a warning of what? That he was nearby and would attack again? Or that his prints led in one direction only – to Cardoroth, and that he would wreak havoc there by way of revenge?

21. The Future is not Fixed

The enemy host was in rampant turmoil, and Gilhain enjoyed it.

"Not since this siege began," he said, "have they been in such disarray."

Aranloth grinned. "No, and it's worse even than it looks."

"How so?"

"Because the elùgroths know that Khamdar returns. And though he failed in his attempt to stop Brand, that does not mean that he will accept *their* failure. He would have hoped that Cardoroth would have fallen by now, and he will blame them that it hasn't, and he is no easy master to serve."

"Why should they fear him?" asked Taingern. "He is only one and they are several?"

"In this case the one is more powerful than the several joined together."

Gilhain scratched his chin. "It poses a question though. Brand is resourceful, but how could he have succeeded with the likes of Khamdar trying to stop him?"

Aranloth looked away. "We always knew that Brand's quest was near impossible. But there is more about him than even you guessed. If we are ever reunited, I think you will see a change in him."

Gilhain did not ask further questions. He caught the faint sense that he was broaching a subject about which the lòhren would not reveal more. Clearly, there was something going on that only Aranloth or Brand knew. Or perhaps only Aranloth. Sometimes the lòhren kept secrets just for the sake of it. Gilhain stopped himself there; that was an unworthy thought. The lòhren said and did what he could. When he kept secrets, there were always reasons for it.

Lornach chuckled. "We're always too serious here. Let's just enjoy the moment instead of analyzing it. What matters most is that we pulled the enemy's beard, and they don't like it – not one bit."

Taingern grinned and put an arm around his Durlin brother.

"That's the truth. Between us all we've disrupted the plans of the enemy more than they ever thought we could. And Jinks has just landed a mighty blow."

"And yet not a killing blow," Aranloth said. "The elug host will suffer in morale and loss of supplies. Hunger will weaken them, but there is still some food, and more supplies will arrive in time."

The lòhren grew more serious as he spoke, not heeding Lornach's suggestion to enjoy the moment. "And make no mistake," he continued. "The elùgroths will drive them on no matter what. They're desperate now. We've won a battle, but we haven't won the war."

Aurellin spoke little at times like these, but when she did, they all listened.

"But what final stroke can there be?" she asked.

There was silence then, and Gilhain felt, one by one, that the gazes of those around began to rest on him. He was the king; he was the great strategist.

"I'm trying to think of one," he shrugged nonchalantly. He made light of it, but the same question burned in his soul and he knew it would run through his mind from now on, day and night, waking and sleeping.

"And do you have any ideas?" Aranloth asked.

"Nothing yet."

"Nor I," the lòhren said quietly.

It was not long afterward that the elùgroths came. There were three of them, and behind each was a shazrahad, the strange elders of the Azan people who fought with the elugs.

Slowly they walked. Their black robes were so dark that they seemed to absorb all light, yet their skin, pale and sickly, stood out all the more for its contrast. But there was little skin to see; the robes covered all except for hints of their grim faces and their bare hands that gripped tight the wych-wood staffs.

They stopped before the wall, and stood motionless. The silence on the battlement was vast. Into that silence their leader spoke.

"Come forth, old man."

No one doubted who he meant. It could only be Aranloth.

The lòhren stepped to the edge of the rampart, and he leaned casually against it. Slowly, insolently, he winked at his three adversaries. They were, perhaps, too far away to see it, but they could not have missed his overall mannerism, nor the contempt that dripped from his voice when he answered.

"Have you come to thank me for my little show? If I don't say so myself, it was impressive. Especially given that it was all illusion. But the elugs believed it, and that was what counted in the end."

Gilhain held his breath. The lòhren was deliberately insulting the enemy, challenging them. It was the sort of thing that Brand would do, and suddenly he saw the likeness between the two men. Strange that he had not noticed it before.

The elùgroths scowled. That much was visible even beneath their cowls.

"Your time has come," their leader said. "Khamdar returns. He nears, and so too does the end of Cardoroth."

116

Aranloth scratched his chin. "I've heard that kind of thing before. And I've heard of Khamdar. He has some notoriety. But you three? I don't know you. Come back and talk to me in a thousand years or so – if you're still alive."

The elùgroths made no move, but enmity radiated from them in waves. If hatred alone could destroy, then the Cardurleth would have crumbled to dust.

Aranloth laughed. "I will give to you a warning," he said. "You seem to think that Khamdar's return is something to worry about. Know this!"

Suddenly the lòhren was not casual any more. He stood straight and tall and the very air about him seemed charged with eldritch forces. It was one of those rare moments when he revealed the power that was in him, and the elùgroths backed away several paces.

"I am more than a match for Khamdar," the lòhren declared. But he is not destined to die by my hand, though die he will, and he will wither in flame and great anguish. You, on the other hand, have no particular destiny. I could snuff you out even as we speak."

Aranloth pointed at them with a white-robed arm, and they stepped back yet again.

"Parley!" they cried. "We come as messengers!"

Aranloth lowered his hand, but his voice rose and swept out, out to the elùgroths and beyond to their army.

"Dogs!" his great voice boomed. "Begone. I will not kill you, at least not now. But beware of Khamdar. You are more likely to die at his hands, for he suffers fools not lightly, and you have failed him. The tide now turns. Cardoroth stands, and the black mass of your host shall recede as the sea before unassailable cliffs."

Aranloth seemed to stand even taller. About him was a flicker of white light, pale silver as the moon, piercing bright as the midday sun.

"Go!" the lòhren commanded, and the elùgroths fled. The shazrahads ran behind them, stumbling and tripping in their flight.

The moment passed. Gilhain let out a long breath, and then he gave a slight bow to the lòhren.

"That was a nice performance. Even as Jinks has seeded doubt and mistrust into the enemy, you have given greater hope to our own men who defend the walls. Even *I* believed what you said about Khamdar. But in truth, I think there are none in Cardoroth who can kill him if it is not you, but that will also keep the enemy thinking and worrying."

Aranloth seemed normal once more. The power that was in him was hidden again, but the remnant of it still lingered in his eyes.

"It was no act. I saw him. In fire and anguish he shall die. And the other elùgroths with him. I gave fair warning to them. They are in great danger, but they will heed me not."

Gilhain did not know what to make of that. The lòhren's manner was strange. But he had seen this mood on his friend before.

"Really? You saw the future?"

Aranloth looked away, his bright eyes surveying the host on the ground below, but his expression was one of deep thought.

"I saw one of them."

"Is there more than one?"

Aranloth looked back. His eyes were an old man's now, and his posture subtly different.

"Of course. There are many, but as the future draws near, the possibilities dwindle. Things become more certain, and most definitely harder to change. I see glimpses of what may yet be from time to time. Some never come to pass, though many do. The future is not fixed as many believe, but events gather pace now, and Khamdar's future and our own, whatever they be, rush now upon us. It is just that there are now fewer possibilities. Two only now remain, most likely."

"But it's better that you saw Khamdar die than us."

Aranloth sighed. "It was good to tell the enemy that. But I must say to you that I have also seen Cardoroth fall to ash and firebrands, and the booted foot of Khamdar on your slain body while he proclaims his victory to the heavens."

22. Stealth

Long days and long nights passed. The Halathrin kept a keen guard, but no further attack was made against the group.

"Khamdar hastens," Harlinlanloth said one morning as they all prepared to set out again.

"How can you tell?" Brand asked.

"The length of his strides has increased. That means he is walking faster."

Brand was not much of a tracker, but he understood that. He also knew that there were no other tracks: the elugs and hounds had scattered and were no longer under the elùgroth's control. Either that, or their master had sent them elsewhere, perhaps even sent them to flank their pursuers and come against them from behind in another attack.

Brand studied the ground. The imprint of the elùgroth was clear, the drùgluck sign clearer still.

"What of his servants?" he asked. "Where do you think they've gone?"

The girl shrugged. "As you already guess, they may have fled, or they may yet seek to ambush us. There's no way to know."

"Small wonder that your scouts are anxious."

She smiled at him. "You couldn't track a bear up a snow slope, but you don't miss much else of what's going on. My people are on the alert for an attack from behind as much as the front, and rest assured, they will not be taken by surprise."

Kareste joined them, leading her saddled horse. "You both worry too much. Khamdar knows of the skills of the Halathrin." She turned to Harlinlanloth. "Your people have better sight and hearing than men. No elug is going to sneak up on you, and not likely the hounds either. Khamdar knows that, and that's why he hastens. He has nothing to fear from our little band. But if his army has taken Cardoroth, then when he reaches them he will turn the whole lot loose to find us."

That was a disturbing thought, and not one that Brand had really considered before. In his heart he knew that Cardoroth still endured, but if not, the small group around him was heading toward the biggest ambush in history.

"What do you think, Harlinlanloth?"

The Halathrin girl tugged absently at her hair. "It could be even as she suggests, Brand of the Duthenor."

"That's a cumbersome title. Just call me Brand."

She let her hair go and smiled. "Brand it is then, Brand."

He laughed. "And I think I'll just call you Harly."

She gave a bow. "A short name for one who has lived as long as I, for we Halathrin tend to gather names to us as the years pass rather than discard them. But I like it."

Kareste mounted her horse and began to move forward. She did not say anything. The Halathrin formed up their travelling positions: some to the front, some to either side, and some behind. One loped far ahead and disappeared. He would scout for them.

Brand and the Halathrin girl stayed in the middle of the group, and she strode beside his horse.

"It's long since I've been here," she said. "But we must be close to a great lake."

"We are," he answered. "Lake Alithorin is close. Its southern shores are only a little way over there." He pointed the direction with Aranloth's staff. "That means

121

we're somewhat hemmed in," he paused before going on. "Perhaps we should stop following the elùgroth's trail. We know where he's going, but if we continue to follow, our enemies will find us all the sooner."

The morning passed, and Brand was undecided. To their left marched the flank of the forest that surrounded the lake. It was dark and silent. To the right were more open lands. Behind lay many things that he would rather forget, and ahead was danger.

Danger. It was a feeling he knew all too well. It seemed that since his childhood he had always been pressing forward against it. He was sick of that fight, sick of pushing against the unknown, of taking on enemies and finding ways to defeat them. One day he would lose, for though he had more luck than most, a time came for every man to die. And the more he pushed the sooner that day was likely to come.

Did he really have to go to Cardoroth? Had he not already played his part? Surely not even Aranloth or Gilhain could ask more of him than he had already given. And the diamond, the massive diamond the king had given him was a just reward. He was a rich man, a man who could find a life of ease and pleasure in other places besides Cardoroth.

The morning passed in silence, and he turned his mind to what troubled him most. There was power in him, magic that he had not asked for nor wanted. He guessed it had always been there, a latent thing that maybe gave him greater insights from time to time and helped him survive his encounters with sorcerers before. Perhaps that was not such a bad thing. While latent he was still in control, but magic had a life of its own, for it came from the land. Aranloth had seen it in him, and put him in a position where it had a chance to come to the fore.

122

Thinking about things, this quest may not have been the first time that the lòhren had done that.

But things were different now. The power inside him had been used, used consciously and deliberately. It was awake, and not easily, if it all, would he be able to suppress it. One thing he knew for sure was that if he went ahead he would be forced to use it again to try to survive. And that would give it greater power, bring it closer to the surface. Even now he felt it run through his body as he considered it. It was a part of him, linked to his body and mind, yet he knew that in some strange way that he was just as much linked to it. It was an entity of its own, and now that it woke it placed thoughts in his mind, gave him knowledge and instincts of how to use it. How else could he have learned so fast and contended with the creatures that he had, and lived?

He brooded on this a long while as he rode. The Halathrin loped at a matching pace, easily maintaining it the whole morning. At times they ranged out, at other times they closed in, all depending on the terrain.

As Brand worried these ideas around in his mind the same way that a dog might gnaw at a bone that had long since been stripped of flesh, a new thought occurred to him. To where could he run to avoid his fate? If Cardoroth fell, which city would be next? The enemy wanted them all, would destroy everything in the north if it could. The more he ran from things the faster might they catch up with him. It was something to think about, for no one knew were the enemy in the south would strike next.

The Halathrin gathered in close. It was noon, and it was time for a rest and a meal. The horses needed a spell also, for it seemed that they tired more easily than the Halathrin. Brand was sure the immortals could keep on going for the rest of the day.

123

They stopped on a small hillock. It had a rocky outcrop at its top and a litter of boulders and loose stones spilled over its near-barren sides. From here, they could see far. On the other hand, they could also *be* seen. Every decision had consequences, and there was rarely a wrong or a right way to do things, just an acceptance of which consequences were preferable.

They finished their meal and then remained silent. They all knew a decision must be made, and they waited on the outcome.

Harly spoke first. "We cannot keep following the elùgroth," she said. "We know where he is going, and we should not make ourselves targets by staying on his trail."

"Agreed," Brand said. "But where shall we head? To the left of his trail or to the right?"

Harly looked him in the eye. "We should go to the right. The lands are open there, and we cannot be ambushed."

Kareste shook her head. "We should go into the forest to the left. We can hide there and sneak close to the enemy host unobserved."

Harly kept her gaze on Brand. "That is an unwholesome forest. It is dark, it has always been dark, and I sense that it is still so. There are many stories of that place, some from of old when my people dwelt there. Dangers lurk amid the shadowy trees, and it would be hard to guard against ambush."

So the argument went for some time, back and forth between Kareste and Harly. At length, they grew quiet.

Harly kept her steady gaze on Brand. "You lead us. It is your choice. You have heard the arguments for and against. You lead, and we shall follow."

Brand sat on a slab rock. The day was dark and gloomy. The clouds above were heavy and pregnant with rain, but none fell yet. That would change, he knew.

He considered things. Was life always like this? So many choices? And each choice had consequences, and he could not see them all.

Nevertheless, he looked at the situation logically. Their small band could not launch a frontal assault on the enemy host. They must work by stealth. And though to the right felt better, to the left offered the concealment of the forest. It offered what they had most need of: secrecy and the ability to come into reasonable proximity of the enemy without being seen.

He made his choice, and he felt better for having done so.

"We go into the forest," he said, agreeing with Kareste. Harly showed little emotion, though he sensed that she was taken aback by the decision. Still, she was as good as her word and without further argument prepared her band to fulfill his choice. Kareste said nothing, but he felt her brown-green eyes searching his face.

The group began to move once more, and they turned left into the forest. The Halathrin stayed close now, and none of them ranged out. Nor was there a scout. Harly herself spear-headed their progress, and they moved at a walk once they passed the tree-line.

The day wore away and they rode toward the vast expanse of Lake Alithorin. Harly led them along a path so faint that Brand doubted anyone but a Halathrin could have found it.

The trail, such as it was, snaked to and fro. It did not seem to head anywhere in particular, but it always took them deeper into the tall stands of pine. It swiftly grew dark beneath the tree canopy, and the air was humid and pungent with the fresh smell of pinesap and the fetid odor of decomposition. Bright orange fungus flowered in lush growths on fallen trunks and hoary lengths of gray-green moss trailed from overhead branches.

The travelers slowed even more. Here, in the shadowy dark amid the trees, it felt like another world. And not a pleasant one.

Brand swayed in the saddle to avoid a low hanging trailer of moss.

"There's definitely something creepy about this place," he said quietly to Kareste.

She ducked under the same trailer of moss. "Woods are woods."

"Not in this case, they aren't. There are things in this forest to fill you with fear. At least as much as Khamdar."

She gave him a sideways look, an appraising kind of glance, but did not answer.

Not long later Brand saw the first signs of fog. There was always fog near the lake, and it contributed as much to the gloomy feelings of the forest as the shadowy paths beneath the trees.

The fog reached out, drifting from the water and stretching forth groping tendrils amid the tree trunks. Moisture clung in a film over the pine leaves and dripped from their needle-like ends. It was deathly quiet, and they saw no wildlife.

It grew darker still. Not because the woods thickened, but because the barely seen clouds far above became heavier and deeper. The silence became so oppressive that Brand felt the need to talk loudly. Yet he dared not talk at all, for who knew what was about them, watching even now, or that would be drawn by the sound of his voice?

And then the rain began. It was soft at first, little more than the fog that already creeped around them. But soon it increased. At last there was a sound, but it was only the drip-drip noise of water drops falling from the ends of leaves.

The leaf mould soon grew muddy, and the smell of fungus and decay grew strong. Even the dark green leaves of the pines looked mournful, and the wet trunks of the trees took on the appearance of a host of tall warriors, grim and determined.

Just on dusk the weather turned even worse. The rain became heavy, and though its intensity varied, it did not remit. It was a bad night, being both wet and cold, and the morning after was no better.

The rain was too heavy to travel, but they had to do so anyway. By mid-morning it had grown even heavier, and instead of becoming lighter beneath the trees as the sun climbed, it was gloomy as a midwinter's night.

The rain fell in waves, and each one seemed a greater downpour than the last. The earth beneath their feet had turned to mud, but they struggled forward, heads down, plodding away relentlessly.

The attack came in the midst of it all. Elugs loomed to the left, springing out of the tree-shadows. There were perhaps twenty of them. From the right several beasts leaped, howling suddenly as they sprang.

Even the Halathrin, the best scouts in the world, gave no warning under the terrible conditions. Their skills were rendered near useless by the weather, and they were as surprised as Brand and Kareste.

Yet the Halathrin reacted quickly. Those nearest the elugs drew their weapons swiftly, and they met the attack with fierce determination. The beasts went for Brand and Kareste, for they slipped between the unprepared Halathrin and came straight at their target.

Brand drew the blade of his forefathers, and it glittered coldly in the dim light. But at the same time fire sprang to the tip of Aranloth's staff. The power in him came unbidden now at times of danger, and he knew he would never be able to stop it from doing so. All he could do was use it sparingly, that would be the key. By doing so he might be able to ensure that he used the magic rather than that it used him. But he had no time to worry about such things.

A hound leapt at him, and his instinct with his sword was stronger than his awakening knowledge of magic. He swayed to the side, his arm loose and relaxed, and he slashed the full length of the sharp blade along the creature's belly.

Blood sprayed from the hound. When it landed, its entrails slipped and gushed from its belly over its legs. It tried to turn and leap again, but it stumbled, its black-clawed paws caught up in a mess of gore and intestines. Brand spun away from it. It was dead even if it did not know it yet.

Kareste sent a ball of fire flying into another hound. It pranced to the side, but the lòhrengai still caught it a glancing blow and in a moment the ruff of fur around its neck caught fire. It howled, a terrible sound from so close, and would have attacked anyway, but Kareste kicked it in the head even as it voiced its pain. It writhed on the ground, but did not get up again. Together they faced the remaining two hounds.

Brand was slower to act. Kareste sent a sheet of fire at them, and it caught them full on. They fell, rose to their feet again, their hair alight, and then they yelped and rolled on the wet earth. Brand stepped toward them, the flame on Aranloth's staff flickering silvery-white in the gloom, but the beasts came to their feet and fled.

Kareste and Brand turned around, but the Halathrin needed no help. A dozen elugs lay dead and the rest were disappearing into the shadowy forest from where their attack had started just moments ago.

The pine woods were quiet except for the receding noise of their attackers as they fled.

In the ensuing silence Harly held up her hand. The rain had momentarily eased, and without the noise of it they heard another sound: the beat of war drums.

"We're close," Harly said quietly.

"Yes," Brand answered. "Closer than I thought. It's hard to find landmarks in this forest."

Kareste came forward. "The rain doesn't help, either. But something has happened. Can't you hear it?"

"Hear what?" Brand asked. "I can hear the drums."

She shook her head adamantly. "Yes. The drums. But listen. Can't you tell the difference? There are far *fewer* of them?"

Brand tilted his head and listened carefully. "You may be right. But it's hard to tell. Everything seems muted within the forest."

"Something has happened," Kareste insisted. "There are fewer drums. Much fewer – I swear it. I don't know what's been going on, but *something* has happened. I guess this much at least – the enemy has not had everything their own way."

Brand did not know about that. He was not sure of the drums either, but if she said so, he believed her. But for once, he was glad to hear the drums anyway, either lots of them or few of them. For it meant the siege still continued. Cardoroth still defied the enemy, and had not gone under.

He turned to Harly. "I'm sorry. Perhaps we should have done what you advised. The forest turned out more dangerous than I expected."

She smiled at him. "Maybe. Maybe not. But this much I think is true. These elugs and beasts weren't the same as the ones we saw with Khamdar. I don't think he sent them here to wait in ambush in case we came this way. I think they were just a patrol, and we were unlucky enough to come their way. It was bad luck, and we could just as easily have had the same kind of ill-fortune if we had gone the way I suggested. There are sure to be patrols all around the enemy host, and we could have run into them no matter where we went."

They pushed on soon after. The rain grew heavy again, and as they moved along it seemed to Brand that they were like mist-phantoms moving through a wet forest. The Halathrin were almost invisible, and they made no noise. Soon, he knew, they would reach a point where they could look out and see the enemy.

But what then? Dare he put into action the plan that was slowly forming in his mind?

23. Why do they Wait?

The beat of drums, of elug war drums – of hate and malice and fear, snaked through the air and up to the Cardurleth. But to be sure, the drums were far fewer than they once were, and their clamor had a thready sound to it like the heartbeat of an old man upon whom death crept near; like, in fact, the pulse Gilhain heard thrum in his chest when he overexerted himself.

The drums were at the heart of the superstitious elug nation. Gilhain knew this, as did all Alithoras. But Aranloth had recently told him more. The lòhren had traced their origin for him, back into the prehistory of the elug race. It was lore that only the lòhrens would possess, and the elùgroths, of course. Those two opposing forces who went back as far as the elugs, or farther, themselves.

The drums were in the blood of the elugs, a part of their race-memory. They predated by far the Halathrin exodus into Alithoras. The unceasing beat was a religion to them, and it marked and measured their life, and the lives of their ancestors back into dark oblivion.

The drums were not just instruments of war. They beat wildly at elug birth ceremonies, and they muttered darky at elug burials. The drums were the heartbeat of their life, and there were words and meanings in their rhythm and tone beyond human comprehension. Small wonder that they were also tools of the elùgroths, implements of control, for the sorcerers ruled all in the south with an iron grip and had long since usurped all means of domination in the races subject to them.

The drums thrummed now before the Cardurleth, fewer by far, and the elugs were disheartened. Gilhain understood better now why that was so. Fear ran among the enemy. Superstition and dread were its companions. The elugs were scared of the riders who had attacked them, brought low their drums and returned in fire and storm into the fortress from whence they had come. They were terrified of another such sortie, and they feared just as much being sent to attack themselves.

But their greatest fear was the elùgroths, and the elùgroths drove them on. War was inevitable. Attack was inevitable. Death was inevitable, for the sorcerers would not give up. Nor, Gilhain knew, would he have done so in their place. No matter the setbacks that they had received, they still dominated the situation. And when Khamdar returned, their strength would be all the greater. Yet still, there was a sense of desperation among the enemy. A feeling that time was running out.

The enemy host now began to seethe like a swarm of ants below. The elùgroths drove them on, the shazrahads whipped them forward. The horde was imbued with a dark spirit, with the very will of the sorcerers themselves. They prepared now for a great assault, an assault that might never end. Wave after wave of attackers would come without respite, and perhaps even the whole host, charge after charge, was going to be thrown against the Cardurleth. Nothing would be held in reserve.

"It builds and builds without end," Taingern said. "Why do they wait? Why not unleash the storm upon us?"

"Because we feel it, and that's reason enough," Gilhain answered. "The storm builds, and death is in the air, just as a real storm builds in the east."

He pointed to the dark clouds piled deep, cloud upon cloud toward the sea. Bad weather was coming from the ocean, but worse trouble was on the ground before them.

"They will let fear erode our will before they strike, but when they come it will be with thunder and lightning, and their charge will be a gale of bodies, of elug warriors driven by the malice of the elùgroths like leaves before a great wind."

Aurellin clenched her fists. "And they do something else also. To reduce us, and to fortify themselves. Look! They gather now the dead riders from the field!"

It was true, Gilhain realized. The bodies of the Black Corps littered the ground, for three hundred had left but few returned. Many of their horses were dead also, laying like carrion on the trampled grassland before the Cardurleth. Yet man and horse both began to jerk and twitch.

Gilhain swallowed hard. Dead men rose to their feet. Dead horses heaved up off the ground to stand on trembling legs. Blood seeped from mortal wounds. Cold entrails spilled from the bellies of horses.

The men pulled arrows from their bodies and let them fall. They straightened broken limbs. All the while they made no sound.

At length, the riders mounted. Slowly, unhurriedly, but with great precision they formed a wedge and took up a position before the Cardurleth, before the Arach Neben, the gate that in life they sought but never reached.

And when the riders found and held their position, though they were silent, the elugs voiced their age old battle-cry that had been heard before cities had fallen for long ages in Alithoras:

Ashrak ghùl skar! Skee ghùl ashrak!
Skee ghùl ashrak! Ashrak ghùl skar!

The chant flowed ceaselessly. It had neither beginning nor end. All the while the beating of the drums that remained grew louder and faster. The stamping of boots thundered, and a low rumble filled the cloud-dimmed sky above the horde.

The king knew what the chant meant.

Death and destruction! Blood and death!
Blood and death! Death and destruction!

Gilhain drew himself up. He did not speak. Now was not the time. Yet he would not be cowed. If death had come for him at last, *still* he would not be cowed.

He watched in silence as the enemy brought forth timber gathered from the pine forests that surrounded Lake Alithorin. It was green, and fresh leaves still sprouted from the many twigs and branches left on it. What this was for, he could not guess, but Hvargil's riders carried it fearfully.

Although Gilhain did not know what purpose the ceremony unfolding before him served, and the re-animated corpses of his own riders sickened and troubled him greatly, he noted with some slight satisfaction that Hvargil himself was not there.

The enemy cavalry took their burden of timber, and they circled the dead riders of the Black Corps. It was an eerie thing to see: the living riders gathering round the dead that sat silently upon their slain horses. And the first piled their burden of timber near to the second.

The drums beat faster, and Aranloth stirred. He spoke, his voice subdued, barely a mumble.

"There is a third thing the enemy will yet do."

"What?" Gilhain asked.

"I sense that Khamdar has returned. He is behind this, for the other elùgroths lack both the strength and skill. His power is enormous, his will dark, and his anger great at the loss of Shurilgar's staff. But the other elùgroths aid him."

"What will come next?"

Aranloth either did not hear, or chose not to answer, but he seemed to gather himself in readiness.

The drums beat faster, and their note changed. At the same time, lifting up and soaring from the midst of the dark host, came the sound of elùgroth chanting. It was a deep and strong sound, harsh and unharmonious, but powerful all the same.

"Do they attack us?" Gilhain asked.

Aranloth answered this time. "Not quite," he said. "Not in body at least. But in mind. Watch, if your heart is strong, and you will see."

Gilhain watched. All on the Cardurleth watched.

Smoke roiled from the ground where Hvargil's riders had placed the timber. It churned under the hooves of their horses. Hvargil's cavalry flowed back into the main host and disappeared, but the smoke, and the dead riders, remained.

Sparks gathered on the conifer branches laid on the ground. Black smoke billowed into the dim sky, and from the thickening clouds a drizzle fell. Soon it became rain, falling in torrential waves, but the sparks and growing flames did not go out.

Smoke billowed, thick and choking, into the air. Fire, like a living thing, took hold of the timber. The branches of the conifers seemed to move and thrash, falling in on themselves as the fire consumed them. But from that seething mass the fire flickered, rose and spread. And then, red and wicked, it leapt from dead horse to dead horse, from dead man to dead man.

The horses did not scream. The men did not cry out. They stood in silence while the flames took hold of them.

135

Gilhain wanted to look away, but he could not. The fire sizzled and popped. The heads of some of the men snapped back. Limbs twisted and writhed as the fire played over them. Then, unbelievably, the horses began to trot, flame spraying from their nostrils as their dead lungs breathed out, sparks flying from their hooves.

They were all dead, men and horses both. But they began to rush forward, and though the flame burned with a great heat, it consumed but slowly.

Yet, the fire *did* consume. The riders drew their swords, and the flesh of their hands melded like hot wax onto the hilts. Their hair burned away. Their faces, once proud in life, began to melt. The skin tightened and drew tight about their skulls in smoke and flickering flame. The stench of death filled the air, and it reached even to the top of the Cardurleth. Yet the riders came forward without pause.

The living riders of Hvargil were now out of sight. But the dead riders held everyone's attention. What would they do next?

The wedge before the gate wheeled and turned with precision. It was a mockery of what they did in life, yet the skill remained to them. Gilhain gasped. Was it possible that the spirits of these men were somehow still in their bodies? Surely no mere sorcery, no animation of dead flesh could mimic the hard-earned expertise of the riders?

They came again toward the battlement. Now even the thick hides of the horses smoked and charred. Hair and flesh burned away. Gilhain saw in many places the red muscles and the white-gleaming bones that drove the animals on. He felt sick, but still he watched. Terrible as it all was to behold, he *must* watch, for something would come next. The elùgroths no doubt executed this plan with more in mind than the desecration of the dead.

The horses snorted red fire. The wounds of the dead men seeped steaming blood, and its falling drops hissed in the air before turning to dark smoke. All along the Cardurleth the men watched in horror. They were silent and pale. They had no words to voice their fear or disgust. Some vomited over the walls. Some fainted. Gilhain gritted his teeth and waited. There was nothing else he could do.

And then the dead riders gathered pace. Swift they came now. The war drums beat with frenetic glee, and behind the wedge of riders the elug horde broke into a charge, screaming in maddened rage, filled and fueled by the sorcerous will of the elùgroths.

24. Have I not the Right?

Brand stood with the others. It was dark, but they had come to the fringe of the forest. The shadowy woodlands lay behind them, and ahead was Cardoroth. The people he loved were close, and the sight of the city that he called home brought a film of tears to his eyes. It was not his home by birth, but he had grown to love it even so.

The city was vast, but it was so gloomy that he could barely see it. It was day time, but the dark clouds had gathered thickly and they unleashed their burden of rain in great torrents.

Out of that darkness came a flash of light. It was all silver and white, and the brightness illuminated much that he could not see before. The enemy host stood out, and the Cardurleth, all of red stone as was much of the city. It seemed that the walls were smeared in blood, and perhaps they were, but they looked like that all the time. It was not a pretty sight, but he loved it anyway.

The Halathrin gasped. It was an ancient city, but to them it was new. They had not seen it before, and well did Brand remember his own reaction to the red stone when first he saw it.

"It always looks like that," he said, but they gave no answer.

And then, as the light faded, they saw the enemy swarm. The horde commenced an attack against the wall, and even in the gloom and rain-swept air, they could still see the outline of the host as it charged, and dimly they heard the wild yells and cries of a maddened foe. Like a deeper shadow amid the gloom it seethed forward, a thing of deep darkness that would swallow the city before it, and then the world after.

There was silence among the watchers. Eventually, Kareste broke it.

"What now?" she asked.

"Now," Brand answered quietly, "I go into the heart of that army, and I find Khamdar and his brethren, and I kill them. If I do that, if I cut the head from the snake, then the army will wither." He paused, allowing his words to sink in, and then he spoke again. "But I do this alone. I don't ask any to come with me."

They looked at him in stunned silence. It was Kareste, once again, who spoke.

"*That* is your plan?"

He shrugged, and then winked at her for good measure. Humor was the best way to deal with fear.

"It's as good a plan as any. And actually it'll be easier than I thought. I hadn't counted on the rain, but that will help conceal me."

"Not once you get close the enemy, it won't."

"I'll also use lòhrengai to make Aranloth's staff and my cloak look black. I think I can do that."

"How quick you are to follow your fate."

"I do what I must … because I must. But after that, we shall see."

"So it always is with you. You do what you must, not what you want. I cannot see the future, but I can see that that will never change. Nor should it, I suppose. That much you've taught me, and much else besides. So, I do now what I also must do. I'll go with you."

Brand shook his head. "No. It'll be easier for one to slip into the enemy army than two. I'll go alone."

Kareste held his gaze. "Would you shame me? Would you make me less than you? You gave up much for me, risked everything on my behalf, and now I do so for you.

139

That also is as it must be. Don't demean my choice by arguing with me. Have I not the right to risk all to help you, as you risked all to help me?"

He *was* going to argue. He was going to find a way to talk her out of it, but he looked back into her eyes and felt the truth of her words. She would not be swayed, and he would only diminish her choice if he tried to.

A long while he looked at her, and a long while she stared back at him. Eventually, he bowed his head slightly, reached out to her and gave her a tight hug.

"You're right," he said. "I don't like it, but you're right, and I'm proud of you. Nevertheless, I won't forgive myself if you get hurt."

The Halathrin watched without speaking, but there was a strange look in their eyes.

Harly eventually approached. When she spoke, her voice was very quiet.

"We also will go with you." She held up the palm of her hand to stop Brand from talking. "We do this for you. But we do it for ourselves and our kind also. Most of all, we do it for Halath, he who died for our people. We understand what you now try to do, for everything you do is for others, even as Halath did. We will follow his example."

He looked at her and slowly shook his head. "Harly, I can't disguise you. You're too fair, too bright, too beautiful to enter the enemy host unobserved. I don't have the skill to change everybody's appearance."

The Halathrin girl smiled at him. "If you have half the skill with lòhrengai that you have at flattery, you could do it with ease. But it doesn't matter. This is a thing I can do for my band, albeit in my own way."

Brand did not argue. He needed these people just as he needed Kareste. At the same time, he did not want anyone to go but himself. Yet, at the end of the day, he had no right to try to deny them the opportunity to do what they felt in their hearts that they had to do. No more right than they had to deny him.

After a few more moments they formed a column. Brand was at their head, Kareste at the rear and the Halathrin between. They had to leave the horses where they were, and their packs also. But Brand took the diamond that Gilhain had given him. He was not about to leave that behind. Then, solemnly, they left the concealing fringe of trees and marched down the rain-slicked slope toward the enemy camp.

25. The Light Grows Brighter

Aranloth spoke, and his voice carried all over the Cardurleth.

"Take heart!" he commanded. "These are the bodies of those who once were our comrades, but their spirit is gone. Sorcery uses them now, raises them up, puts their feet in the stirrups and makes the horses pace. Remember your brothers for who they were, and know that these are no longer they."

The riders charged. Fire leaped and darted beneath the cold hooves of dead horses. A haze of smoke gathered, and it rose into the air, and the riders rode upon it, angling up into the very air themselves, climbing upon dark sorcery toward the top of the rampart.

The stink of burning flesh was everywhere. The stench of opened entrails accompanied it. The eyes of the enemy, who once were comrades, burned and sizzled in their sockets, staring without emotion or pain, staring inhumanely, staring as the dead horses galloped.

The defenders fired arrows. They hurled spears and javelins. These implements of war stuck in the riders, but the enemy rose higher, rode closer, came on without any interruption. The dead were already dead. Neither death nor pain nor the tactics of battle concerned them.

The horses snorted flame. The riders neared. The skin of their faces peeled away to reveal the haggard grin of death, and flames curled around the white teeth protruding from bony jaws.

Blood spurted from their wounds, falling down, boiling and sizzling like a ghastly rain on the barren earth below.

And then, as the riders approached, it splattered on the stone of the rampart.

Men fled their stations. Suddenly, loud and horrible, was the sound of iron-shod hooves on stone. The smell of corruption was overpowering.

At that moment the lòhrens finally acted, for this was an attack beyond skill and courage of arms. A white light sprang forth. It was soft, silvery, reminiscent of a midwinter moon. But however soft the light started, it swiftly grew and encompassed the riders even as they reached the Cardurleth.

On the rides came, unstoppably. Yet the lòhrengai did not seek to block them, to oppose elùgai with its own might. Instead, it took the force thrown against the city and transformed it. The riders rode, but they continued their upward ascent, being just barely deflected from their destination.

Up they rode. Higher and higher. Up and over the battlement and then above the city beyond. The silvery light grew brighter. And for all the horror unleashed there was now a sense of peace, for the light bathed everything as though the very moon itself hung pregnant with argent beauty in the sky.

The light was no ordinary light. Peace came with it, release and ease of spirit. And hope. Hope most definitely, Gilhain felt. It was unexpected, unlooked for, more powerful than any darkness.

Somewhere far below in the city a bell tolled. And as though that were a signal the light became suddenly blindingly bright. Gilhain cast his eyes downward, and saw at the edge of his vision, or beyond the vision of normal sight, a fleeting glance, faint and shimmery as though from a great distance, of green grasslands and a silver river winding through them.

143

Gilhain thought of the origin of the Black Corps, of the refugees to the city and from the land whence they had come.

Even as he thought of their homeland, the riders now high above gave a shiver in their saddles as they wheeled once more in precision, and then, banking away to the left like a flight of white doves, they disappeared. And the silvery light with them.

Gilhain let out a long breath. They were gone. The light was gone. But a lingering sense of peace remained for a while, but that too, with each beat of his heart, began to fade.

It was dark again. Almost night-dark. Water ran as a sheet over the stone, for at some time that he did not quite realize it had begun to rain in a mighty downpour. Men rushed back to the front of the battlement.

But the enemy host below, driven now by powers beyond recall, swarmed as a dark wave and crashed upon the wall.

26. The Storm Breaks

The nearer they approached, the better Brand saw the unstinting attack of the enemy on Cardurleth. His heart swelled with pride; not just of Gilhain and Aranloth, not just of the Durlin, but also of the everyday soldiers who had defended the city since even before he had left on his quest. They had endured. They had borne attack after attack, suffered horrors that could not be described. And still they stood, awaiting some final hope, hope that for all they knew would never come. But *still* they endured.

He was proud of them. And he felt a great love of the city wash over him. It was always thus, he knew. The greater the danger the more something, or someone, was appreciated. But cities fell even as did people, and he knew in his heart that nothing was permanent. The history of Alithoras taught him that, and his own life had brought home the message even more strongly.

Cardoroth had endured. But nothing lasted forever, not even great courage, and soon, very soon now, the end must come. The city teetered on the edge of fate, and the next few hours would send it into oblivion or light it as a beacon of hope for the whole land.

The small band made their way through the rain, which grew even heavier. Brand reached out with his thought. He drew the downpour about himself and his companions. It whipped and lashed at them, and thereby helped to obscure them from the army they approached.

He felt power, and he felt the lòhrengai that was in him pulse through Aranloth's staff. It was there because he made it so, because he had chosen to wake it, and very gently the staff began to glow. As it did so, he brought his mind to bear, concentrated on the gloom that was about him, and the flicker of silver light turned darker, transformed slowly and surely to black.

Brand thought about what he had done. He had not changed the color of the staff, but merely the light that sprang from it. It was a subterfuge, rather than a real change. He knew, instinctively, as he knew so many other things about lòhrengai, that to make real change, or to create something from nothing, was the hardest thing of all. To take something that already existed, and to transform it, was much easier. But still not easy, for doing such things taxed the mind just as physical effort taxed the body.

The gloom of the dark day, and the rain and the scudding clouds above were all around him. He had used that subdued light, that atmosphere, to bring forth darkness of his own, but he did not stop with the staff. He did the same for his clothes, making them appear black, creating a shadow about himself to make it seem that he wore an elùgroth's cloak.

All the while he heard a soft chanting behind him. The words were in the Halathrin tongue, but they were harsh and guttural and he did not know their meaning, though they seemed tantalizingly familiar.

He turned and looked at the Halathrin. Their once beautiful forms were become grotesque. Fangs sprang from their gray-lipped mouths. Their skin had become gray-green even as that of the elugs. Their limbs were now long and ungainly, and the hair on their heads, spilling from beneath now-tarnished helms, was lank. They wore also the leather jerkins of elugs, the cheap armor stained by blood and grime.

The one at their front leered at him evilly, and with a shock he realized it was Harly. A shiver ran down his

146

spine, and she laughed at him, showing wicked fangs and a lolling red tongue. He suppressed his revulsion and winked at her, which made her laugh all the louder.

He turned to the front again, leader of this band of savages, and pulled about him a sense of menace and power.

Soon, they came to a picket line of miserable elugs with their cloaks wrapped tightly about them and their heads bent low to keep their eyes out of the rain.

Brand did not hesitate. To try to hide, to try to slip through was death. He walked brazenly at them. The elugs looked up at him, and he stared back, and he allowed his hatred of Khamdar, his hatred of the enemy to fill his eyes. He imagined crushing his foes, sweeping them into oblivion with steel and lòhrengai. The elugs saw the look in his eyes, the malice-laden glance of an elùgroth, and backed away.

A path opened, and they went through the gap. And then, within a hundred paces they were within the enemy host itself. Elugs milled all around them. At times, there were Lethrin. Then, suddenly and unexpectedly, he nearly bumped into a man of the Camar race.

Brand hid his shock, for shocked he was. But then he pieced it together. Hvargil must be here somewhere. And that made him wonder what strange things had happened in his absence. For even as much had happened to him, clearly much had happened here also.

He headed toward the center of the host. There they would find the elùgroths. He had no need to try to track them down by guesswork, for he heard sorcerous chanting ahead, and then the voices of hundreds of elugs join in. Some dark elùgai was being worked, and Brand hastened. Already the wall was in danger of falling from the great attack hurled against it, and this new stroke, whatever it was, could mean the end.

He looked up, but could no longer see the bulk of the Cardurleth, only the top of it dimly through the obscuring rain.

The clouds, thick banks of black and deep-sea blue that piled one upon another, roiled ominously. A storm was about to break, and Cardoroth was at its center. There was a boom of thunder, and it was not sorcery. Nature was about to unleash its fury, uncaring of man or elugs, peace or battle. And about the edges of the storm jagged shafts of lightning flashed and leaped, spearing toward the earth as though the sky made war upon the earth.

Ahead, Brand finally saw the elùgroths. Soldiers cowered motionless about them, crouching low to try to shelter themselves. Brand and his small group were all that moved, all that dared to move when it seemed that the fury of the sky would break the world apart.

On Brand strode. On his band came behind him. None stood in their way, for all scattered at his approach and he felt the fear that elùgroths generated among those they led. It sickened him, but the power of it fueled his pride also. For the first time he knew what every lòhren had felt before him: temptation. And he knew he must always be on his guard. Power was a lure, a trap for the unwary, a golden path that led to blackness. Better now did he understand what Kareste had gone through.

On he walked, and fear stabbed at his heart like the lightning that seared the ground. Here was Khamdar, and he was not alone. His brethren were with him, and a horde of elugs and dark foes at the sorcerer's beck and call.

Brand slowed. His heart turned to ice, and he knew at this moment that death was likely, nearly certain, and that life and hope were as distant from him as clear skies and bright sunlight.

He faltered, and he sensed the fear of those behind him like a wave. This was madness. This was suicide. This was stupidity. Maybe, just maybe, they could yet turn around and leave the host even as they had entered it.

A buffet of cold wind slapped him in the face, but he did not feel it. His mind raced, but as it did so he thought of all those who had died by Khamdar's hand. And how many defenders of Cardoroth had fallen? And what if the city succumbed? Perhaps, just perhaps, he could prevent that, or at the least hinder the enemy. If he died, it might be better than living with the guilt of not trying to protect those he loved. Not just Gilhain and the Durlin, not just Aranloth. But the people of Cardoroth, the women and children who might yet see the sun shine again, even if he would not.

Brand made his choice and strode forward again. Like a wave, the others followed in his wake, drawn forward by the strength of his will. They all went now to their deaths, but they went with one purpose, and they went as brothers and sisters to meet their fate.

They saw the elùgroths more clearly. Lightning flared and crashed all around them. In its flickering light, the dark forms of the sorcerers were clear. They sat in a wedge, their wych-wood staffs held in their laps, their voices rising in a chant of dark magic, of magic that one way or another would be hurled at the city they strove to destroy.

And beyond, illuminated by the same fitful light, was the Cardurleth. The enemy swarmed against it, engulfed it as a dark tide. How could the defenders hold? Yet hold they did.

Brand felt something smash against his arm. And then something else struck his shoulder. It was hail, and it felt as though the very sky began to hammer the earth and all who stood upon it.

The elug host wailed. The massive Lethrin wrapped their arms about their heads. Brand strode on, and the elùgroths kept chanting.

The hail grew much larger and fell in a heavy blanket. As swiftly as it started it faltered, and then, just as swiftly again, it fell once more. This time the hail-stones were even larger, and they fell so thick that the ground was become white and the noise of their battering was a roar in Brand's ears.

But on he strode, and his band followed. They were near the elùgroths now, but they were also near the Lethrin who stood adjacent as an honor guard. And the Lethrin looked and watched, their heads coming up despite the hail, and their hands reaching down for weapons.

At the very end, Brand had been discovered. To fool elugs was one thing, but the Lethrin who guarded the sorcerers was another. They knew better than the rest of the army who their masters were, and what they looked like.

Brand stared at them, hatred and power in his eyes, emulating the elùgroths. But the Lethrin could not be deceived. They were about to sound an alarm, but the Halathrin were already acting. Their bright swords glittered amid the gloom, flashing like little streaks of lightening.

Brand and Kareste raced toward the elùgroths. There were only six left, for evidently they had not had things all their own way during the siege. But it was still a fight of three to one, and Brand did not like those odds.

They had not reached them when the elùgroth at the head of the wedge looked back, alerted by the sudden noise and mayhem behind him. It was Khamdar, and even as he looked Brand saw swift recognition in the other's eyes.

Khamdar cried out in a tongue that Brand did not understand, but the rest of the elùgroths obviously did. They lurched to their feet, their chanting forgotten, and hatred burning like fire in their dark eyes.

27. Burn!

The elùgroths spread out. Khamdar was on their right, and it was toward him that Brand looked. Kill the leader, and the followers would flail about like a headless snake.

Khamdar, for all that he was taken by surprise, acted with speed and determination. Crimson fire spurted from his staff. The sorcerous flame flashed through the air. Rain sizzled. Steam billowed upward. But Brand was ready, and he held Aranloth's staff before him, and his drawn Halathrin blade also.

The attack struck, and Brand took that power, felt the skill and strength that lay behind it, and managed to deflect it upward until it pierced the dark clouds above.

He did not wait where he was, but sprang forward. If he were to have a chance against Khamdar he must not fight him on the elùgroth's own terms, elùgai against lòhrengai. He must bring his sword to bear, use his skill as a warrior. It was a small advantage, and it could not compensate for the disadvantage of fighting someone far more powerful, but it was all he had.

Khamdar struck again. The hail that lay on the ground between them seethed and rose into the air. It coalesced, and then like an arrow shot at Brand.

Brand had no answer to that. Not with lòhrengai, but he did not need to. He dived and rolled, coming up again many yards from where he had stood. Still, he felt the whoosh of air by his body as the ice-arrow sped past him. And then he heard screams from the elug camp behind as the sorcerous attack killed unintended victims.

But Khamdar did not care. His cloak billowed about him as he moved in closer himself, driving toward Brand even as Brand came toward him. That was off-putting, for it showed that the sorcerer feared neither staff nor blade.

From the left, Brand saw lights flicker. Kareste was in a battle of her own, but he dared not take his eyes of his enemy. That was death.

A ring of crimson fire sprang up around him. It began to swirl, but even as it did so Brand reached out with his thought. He joined his power to that of the elùgroth's. The fire intensified, and the whirling increased. The air about Brand shimmered with heat, but the whirlwind of fire lifted up from the earth and soared away into the roiling sky.

Rain dripped down Brand's face. His body was covered in sweat. He felt chilled to the bone, for this was a life and death struggle. But he took heart.

Somewhere behind him now the Halathrin battled the Lethrin, and that fight continued. So too did Kareste's struggle. Light and fire sizzled from her direction, and he saw the crumpled forms of several elùgroths.

Brand and Khamdar closed. His Halathrin blade gleamed with lòhrengai. He cut and thrust, but Khamdar spun to the side, and like a whip his wych-wood staff came down. It struck Brand on the face, and he reeled back.

Pain shot through him. Anger rose. In a fury he leaped forward. Aranloth's staff was forgotten. He attacked with his blade, and he drove in, swinging, sweeping and stabbing in a mad rush. But for all the speed of his attack, it was not without skill. Every move was calculated. Every technique honed by years of practice and fighting experience.

But he did not break through the elùgroth's defenses. The sorcerer was like a shadow, and no matter how fast Brand was, he could not get ahead of him. Yet still,

Khamdar had an opportunity to attack himself. He dodged and leaped, his every thought bent on staying alive.

But, as Brand knew he must, he began to tire. And that was the moment that the sorcerer had waited for.

Khamdar struck with great speed. He had learned his lesson previously and did not speak or taunt. He raised his staff in his right hand, but it was from his left, held low, that fire spurted.

Like jagged lightning it hissed, sizzling and steaming through the air. Brand ducked, but not quick enough. A vicious blow caught him on the shoulder and sent him staggering back. His cloak burned, and smoke spiraled upward.

Some instinct long dormant within him rose to the surface. Before he could even think about it his mind reached out and pushed the fire away, but Khamdar was not done.

The sorcerer now sent flame from his staff as well, and Brand spun further back. He fell to the ground, and then rose again. A nimbus of silver light shone from within him, protecting him against the attack. Yet he was tired in both body and mind.

His protection faltered. He swayed on his feet, and the attack against him intensified. Suddenly, a figure was leaping from the side of his vision. He thought it was Harly, but it was not. It was the Halathrin with the scar who had warned him away from her.

The warrior sped across the muddied earth. Khamdar saw him, and hesitated. Then, he pointed the staff at him and sprayed him with fire. The warrior dove to the ground, but he was hit. He came up again, now between Brand and the sorcerer. He raced in, covered in flames, burning as he ran. Khamdar leaped back and now attacked with both streams of flame.

The warrior screamed. He fell to the ground, but even as he did so he hurled a small dagger.

Khamdar was swift yet again. The dagger burst into flame and shot off to the side to land in the mud, where it smoked and hissed.

The Halathrin warrior did not live to see his attack fail. But Brand was still alive, kept that way by one he had thought was not his friend.

Brand used the brief moment of respite wisely. He reached out with his thought, conscious this time of what he was doing, and drew the rain about him as a protective shield.

Khamdar drew himself up. Slowly he walked toward Brand, and fire spurted from hand and staff. The new attack knocked Brand backward again, but somehow, he kept his footing.

Brand struggled to move forward to meet his enemy, but Khamdar laughed.

"You are outmatched, fool."

Brand made no answer, and he took another step forward.

Khamdar shook his head. "You are dead, but you know it not. Watch then! Learn what true power is, for I am greater than you, and my skill, honed long ages before you first drew breath, is beyond the reach of your thought."

The sorcerer drew himself up. Tall he stood, and terrible. Blackness was about him, and it was not the gloom of the storm that raged all around them. It was a blackness of spirit. Brand felt as though he looked over the edge into a bottomless pit. And thither, into the great dark, he knew he must fall.

"Burn," Khamdar said. "I foretold that you would perish in flame and anguish, and thus it comes to pass. Burn!"

And Brand felt the full force of his enemy's will. It was a crushing power, greater than his own, steeped in malice that itself struck him as a blow over and beyond the sorcery.

The protection that Brand had drawn about himself was stripped away. Water sprayed up and outward. He stood there, so tired it was all he could do to stay on his feet. Some last instinct flickered to life and a silver-white nimbus surrounded him. He knew that he could not last long, that this protection would also be taken from him.

"Burn!" the elùgroth screamed.

Scarlet flame swept through the air. It sent Brand spinning. Somehow, he again stayed on his feet. Somehow, the nimbus survived, but it flickered fitfully, nearly gone as was Brand's will to live. There was only so much a person could endure, and he knew he had gone past his limits.

"Burn!" Khamdar said again. His voice was quieter this time, but the will behind it even stronger. The elùgroth waxed in power as he saw his enemy succumb.

Brand felt the nimbus of power about him die. With a final flicker it went out, but then, beyond his comprehension, Kareste was before him, protecting him. Somehow she had survived, abandoned or won her own battle, and she was come to his aid.

But that hope was short lived. She was as exhausted as he. With a negligent flick of his wych-wood staff Khamdar sent a stream of flame at her that knocked her down to the muddied earth. But he did not follow up on that attack. He looked again at Brand.

"I will kill her when I am done with you."

Slowly, the elùgroth walked toward him. As though from a great distance Brand heard fighting behind him. The Halathrin still engaged the lethrin. There could be no help from them.

156

Brand was outmatched, outfought, and he knew it. Too young was he in his power, too unskilled. He had no choice but to wait for death, because the power to fight was no longer his.

By some immense force of will he stayed on his feet, unwilling to die on the ground, a beaten and defeated thing. Khamdar was not right: he *was* dead but he *did* know it.

And yet, one last gamble came to his mind. He had not the power to contend with one of the great elùgroths, yet had he not survived thus far by deflecting his enemy's attacks, rather than opposing them force to force? Might not he have one last hope? His instincts had not yet surrendered, and nor would he.

He drew forth from an inner pocket the diamond Gilhain had given him. At the same moment, Khamdar spoke again, and his voice was a command.

"Burn!"

The single word, louder than thunder, cracked the air.

Khamdar levelled his staff. Wicked flame ran along its length, and Brand saw the light of that same sorcerous flame in his enemy's eyes.

The flame leaped. Intense, murderous, bent on his destruction.

Brand welcomed it. He opened his mind, drew it in with his thought. He became one with its roiling fury, but he did not fight it. He did not resist it. He felt its heat, and relished it. He felt its hunger, and knew insatiable desire. He felt its rage, and knew madness. It enveloped him, became his body, and a pillar of wicked flame rose as a towering inferno about him.

And then two other elùgroths staggered toward Khamdar and joined their power to that of their master. The flame intensified. Dimly, Brand heard the roar of flames, the lustful cries of elugs and a single heartbroken scream from Kareste.

All the while he drew in the force that pummeled him, drew it in and guided it into the hard diamond. On it went, relentlessly. The elùgroths showed no mercy. They burned, fueling their elùgai with hatred, spending themselves utterly in their lust for destruction.

But when their strength faltered, when their power one by one drew to an end, Brand was still there. And in his hand the diamond shimmered with trapped power. It was no longer hard in his grip, but soft like clay. He could shape it with his fingers, and he sensed that what had gone into it must come out. It was caught there like a beast in a cage, but there was no substance on earth that could long hold such power trapped.

The last remnant of flame about his body flickered and died. He stood before the elùgroths, unharmed and implacable. His will to live was greater in the end than their will to kill.

Brand stepped toward them. Somewhere behind him lay his sword and staff on the scorched earth. High he held the diamond, and the elùgroths, even Khamdar, were shocked and fearful. They shrank from him.

He heard Kareste gasp in shock, but he did not look at her. His mind was fixed on his enemies, on the enemies of all mankind.

"Thus I cast your curse back into your teeth, Khamdar. Burn. Burn and perish, for there is no place for such as you in the world. Burn and pass from Alithoras, and as you die, think of the many that you killed. Think of them, and feel their vengeance."

Brand released the sorcery caught in the diamond. It leaped out, and like chain-lightning sprang from elùgroth to elùgroth. But the force did not spurt out slowly as it had been gathered in. The release was sudden, and the swift outlet of such power cracked the air more loudly than the thunder of any storm.

The earth trembled. The Cardurleth seemed to sway, and the elùgroths screamed.

Up into the heavens the wailing rose. The lesser elùgroths fell to the ground. Khamdar stayed upright, and he staggered toward Brand, one hand reaching out in supplication or attack. But then he too stumbled and fell.

Brand did not relent. The last of the force stored in the diamond shot outward. The clothes of the elùgroths burned, and their flesh with it. The muscles of their limbs withered away in smoke. Fat flared and dripped like sputtering candles. Their eyes sizzled and smoked leaving blackened holes, and their faces shriveled, revealing the white bone beneath.

The elùgroths died. And their wych-wood staffs turned to a fine ash. All about them the hail still fell, yet where the elùgroths burned the heat was so great that the ice melted. Water ran with blood, and burning streaks of fat hissed and bubbled.

Brand stood there. There had been shock and despair on Khamdar's face before it melted away. And though Brand had seen men die before, had killed many himself, yet still what he had seen would haunt his dreams as long as he lived. But he did not feel sorry for the elùgroths. Justice could be as cruel as any crime, but that did not make it wrong.

The elug host moaned. Brand looked around. He did not know when it had happened, but he had fallen to his knees. Nearby were dead Halathrin, and dead Lethrin also. But still some of the immortals were left alive. Harly was one of them, and she held his gaze a moment. Her eyes were wide and there were emotions in them that surpassed his comprehension. Too much had happened, and he was too weak to stand, let alone think.

But hammering at his vision was something else that finally seeped through to his consciousness. The elug host was fleeing. In a mad rush they ran, abandoning the siege. Their leaders had died in fire and anguish, and the storm raged at them like a living thing. Bereft of the malicious will that had infused them, fear drove them instead.

Brand looked to Cardoroth. From the city came an army. Real, or a phantom of his exhaustion, he did not know, but he could not keep his eyes on it. He fell to the ground and rolled onto his side. From his hand ash scattered, all that was left of the precious diamond.

Dimly, he saw Kareste and Harly run toward him. They reached him and held his hands. He did not at first understand the worried looks on their faces, and then he felt the pain in his chest. He looked down, and saw the hilt of a dagger sticking out from his flesh. An elùgroth dagger, marked on blade and hilt with the drùgluck sign.

Khamdar had killed him, and he had not even seen or felt the dagger thrown by his enemy. But life was sweet. Kareste and Harly were alive. Cardoroth still stood.

He felt the hands of the two girls grip tight his own as oblivion claimed him. Just as it did, though all was dim and shadowy about him, he felt other hands upon him, gentle, firm, skilled. And then there was only darkness.

28. Filled with Power

Not for the first time, Gilhain marveled at the men who defended Cardoroth. They fought against all odds, and without any real hope.

The enemy swarmed the walls. They came without stint, hatred in their battle-cries and madness in their eyes. That madness was born of the elùgroths, of that the king was sure, but however it came to be, it was only its presence that mattered. For the elugs fought with a fury that he had never seen before.

The elugs did not give up. Death swept them aside by the hundreds, but they no longer feared it. They fought as creatures possessed, and when one fell another took its place. So it went, and it seemed without end.

Blood ran over the stone floor of the rampart. Bodies lay there, dead and maimed. Others were maimed but not dead. The living fought for their lives, trampling all that lay beneath.

In contrast to the fury of the enemy, the defenders fought with grim quietude. There was, almost, a sense of peace among them. Perhaps it was really so, for Gilhain still had a lingering sense of tranquility from Aranloth's white light. But be that as it may, with or without Aranloth, the men fought to save and preserve while the elugs fought to destroy. That was in some ways a small difference, and in others enormous. It was, Gilhain knew, a bigger difference than any of the other things that separated them. The men did what they must do, live or die, and hatred did not drive them.

Afar in the city all was silent. The people had gathered in the streets. They watched, but did not talk. The Durlin stood around the king, drawing closer to him for the final confrontation that must come soon, for this could not continue. They guarded him until the end.

Aurellin was there, as she always was. The storm broke, and wind and hail lashed the battlement. It was hard to see, yet still Gilhain sensed that the very air seemed to shiver, to draw back and away from the violence of the storm.

The air shimmered, yet something appeared that was not air or rain or hail. It had the form of a man, though many times larger.

And it was no man, but a devil raised by the elùgroths. Black wings sprouted from its muscular back. Horns, twisted and curved, grew from its massive skull, towering above its head like a crown of evil.

With a bellow as loud as thunder it stepped forth, and the Cardurleth trembled at the weight of its tread. The soldiers scattered. The creature paid them no heed, but came for Gilhain, its eyes burning with the light of hatred.

The Durlin stood before it. But before them stood Aranloth. And he was not as he usually appeared, an old man of uncertain humor and old regrets. He revealed now his full power, showed the might that was in him. For dark as the devil was, wrapped in shadow and evil, the lòhren blazed with an inner light. He would contend with this thing, and even as its shadow fell over him, the devil paused.

Aranloth had no weapon, but the massive beast, a thing of rippling shadow and muscle, drew forth a mighty sword that smoked and flickered with wicked light. The blade was bent, tooth edged and longer than the span of a tall man.

Aranloth cocked his head, but made no move to flee or to attack.

"Stay!" the lòhren commanded. Even as he spoke he held up his hand, palm out.

The beast hesitated, and the shadow and wicked light ebbed and flared uncertainly along the blade of its sword.

Aranloth spoke again, but it seemed that he did not address the devil, but rather those elùgroths who had summoned or made it.

"The moment is upon you," he said. "Choose now, and choose swiftly, if it is not already too late. Pull back, Khamdar. Take your host and go."

Khamdar answered through the beast; through twisted mouth and cruel fang his voice rang out.

"Those are empty words, old man. Your hope is dead. I will kill you, and the glory will be mine. The honor and the praise of he that I serve will raise me unto godhood. Verily, I would not retreat now though the spirits of all those that I have vanquished joined together to kill me. Let them come, for they are dead and I am on the brink of ultimate power!"

"So be it," Aranloth said softly.

The lòhren bowed his head. The beast took a step forward. Aranloth did not move.

Hail beat around the two figures. Lightning flickered and hissed nearby. A sulphurous smell filled the air.

The devil lifted high its sword. Fire darted in its eyes and shadows writhed about it. Its great arm bulged with muscles, and it gripped the black hilt with a taloned hand.

A moment thus it stood, ready to strike. Aranloth waited, and then the creature dropped the mighty blade to the battlement.

There was no noise, no clang, no rattle of metal against stone. The sword ceased to exist the moment the creature let it go.

And then the beast turned and looked behind it. Gilhain watched, rooted to the spot by fear or fascination. Which, he did not know, but he watched.

The devil shape tensed, and the face of the creature showed surprise. Suddenly, it seemed more human. It wavered, great folds of shadow billowing about it as its dark wings trembled, and then it was gone, gone in the blink of an eye as though it had never even existed.

The onrush of elugs faltered. Many had gained the wall because it was unmanned, yet most had held back, just as scared of the devil as were the defenders. No one seemed to know what was happening.

But now men began to come back to their positions, and there was great turmoil in the host below. A light flashed, sharp and bright. Then there were more and more flares and bursts of power. On it went, and it seemed that the world stood still. Only the storm moved, venting its fury, but the two opposing armies seemed paralyzed.

Finally, a burning light, too bright to watch, pierced the rain-thick air, and screams rose up from far below, full of pain and anguish beyond any cry that Gilhain had ever heard. Then a boom rolled across the battlefield as though the earth itself cracked asunder.

The enemy host suddenly moved. At first, everything below seemed a mad panic, but quickly it became evident that the horde was breaking up, scattering, taking flight.

"What's happening?" Gilhain asked.

Aranloth seemed tense, and his eyes were distant. But then he answered.

"More than we could hope. But when you trust in such as Brand, hope is rarely cheated."

"*Brand?*"

"Aye. Brand. He has come, returning to us over the long leagues of Alithoras, and there are others with him.

And they attacked the heart of the enemy, the head of the snake as he would call it."

"The elùgroths?"

"Verily. And rejoice if you can, for death is a bitter thing to all, to evil as much as to good, but they are dead. All of them, including Khamdar. That is why the enemy flees."

Gilhain thought. But not for long. There would be time to rejoice later. For now, he must act. Swiftly he issued orders for the regular cavalry to leave the city and harry the enemy, lest they regroup.

"Tell them to harass the elugs," he instructed the messenger. "Kill them. Give them no peace. Find their supply wagons, or what is left of them, and target them wherever possible."

And then the king watched and waited from atop the Cardurleth. The enemy retreated, and the riders of Cardoroth pursued.

A small group was left in the middle of the field, and suddenly Aranloth's voice rang out.

"Brand is wounded!" the lòhren yelled.

Before those words were finished it seemed that Arell was already moving.

Gilhain did not know what to feel. Somehow, beyond hope, they had won. But at what cost?

Aurellin slipped her hand into his. He bowed his head, and gently squeezed her. She squeezed his hand back.

"Cardoroth will endure," he whispered.

But Aranloth heard him also, and it was the lòhren who answered.

"And yet the shadow is not vanquished. Only its long arm is injured."

The truth of those words struck home to Gilhain. They had won a great battle, but the war was only beginning. It would be fought in other times and places. No doubt, it would be fought here again, even if in another fashion. But his time as king was drawing to an end. Another must soon bear the burden, for he was growing too old to continue as he had done. His time in Alithoras was nearly spent, but there was another to take his place. Another, who was prepared to give his life for all that he loved, if he had not already done so.

29. Can You Deny Her?

Arell knew what she was doing. She had no lack of confidence, no lack of skill, yet still she worried about Brand.

The dagger of the elùgroth had gone deep. The blade had slipped between his ribs. That in itself was unusual, for the ribcage was good at protecting the vital organs of the body; that was one of its purposes. But the blade had apparently not penetrated far enough to touch his heart or damage his lungs.

So far so good. But why was he so ill? She looked up from her ministrations and saw Aranloth and several others had come down from the battlement, but it was the lòhren who was most important just now.

"Do the elùgroths use poison on their daggers?" she asked.

The lòhren shook his head. "That's unlikely. They have no aversion to such a thing, but they have better means of protection at their disposal."

That was good news. But then another thought occurred to her.

"What about sorcery?"

Aranloth frowned. "That's certainly possible," he said. He peered closely at the dagger for a moment, and then knelt down. Tentatively, he reached forward and brushed his fingers against the hilt that protruded from Brand's chest. He did not grasp it though, and Arell saw him flinch as his skin touched it.

Several moments passed, and Arell held her breath. At length, the lòhren stood.

"There is elùgai infused into the blade, but it is not of a kind that would hurt Brand. The spells woven about it are of sharpness and seeking. They are potent, but they would have only helped the blade bite deeper. We can be thankful that whoever threw it had poor aim, otherwise it would have found what it sought."

"And what was that?" Gilhain asked.

Arell answered, thinking aloud more than anything else.

"The heart, no doubt. And it was close too, but Brand's luck has always been good."

"That's exactly right," Aranloth confirmed. Though whether he was talking about the dagger or Brand's luck, Arell was not sure. Perhaps both.

"Then I think I know what the trouble is," she said. "He's exhausted. Exhausted to the point of death, as only a man with the will of Brand can drive themselves. And the dagger, though not the main problem, could well push him over the edge."

"What then is the treatment?" the king asked.

"I'd like to get him back into the city where I can do things properly, but he may not survive that long. So, I'll draw the dagger out here. If he survives that, then his body can start to heal, and then he may regain some strength."

"Do as you must, Arell," the king said. "I have confidence in you."

Arell did not answer. She had spoken in matter of fact tones. It was her job to do so, for it gave confidence to those who watched the treatment. But most of all, it brought to the fore that part of her mind that analyzed and assessed, that diagnosed and initiated treatment, and by concentrating on that it kept the other part of her mind that felt and feared, suppressed. And just as well, for if her emotions got loose on her she would fall to pieces. She could not let Brand die!

Swiftly she made her preparations, dabbing an unguent around the wound that would help protect against infection. She prepared cloth, in case of bleeding, and then she put both her hands to the hilt of the dagger. She must be steady here.

She took a deep breath, and then she gradually let it out, withdrawing the dagger very slowly at the same time.

Brand moaned as the blade began to move. She gave a curt nod, and several sets of hands immediately pressed down upon him to keep him still so that he could not hurt himself.

The blade slipped free, but it was not easy. Wounds were often like that; extra blood and tense muscles put pressure on blades that made it so.

The dagger was a wicked looking thing, and it dripped with Brand's blood. Swiftly she put it down and inspected the wound.

She could see little, and had no way to know if there was dirt or other foreign material in there. If she had time and leisure, she would have considered trying to clean it, but that had its own dangers, because no matter how careful a healer was, there was always the chance of introducing foreign material that had not been there before. Often, whatever caused infections was so small that it could not even be seen.

Arell resorted to what had often worked well for her in the past. She drenched the wound with a special fluid. She gave her clients a long-sounding name for it, but the king and the Durlin knew it was merely a kind of potent spirit brewed by those who had no taste for wine or beer. Many healers would use wine for such a purpose, but she had found that the spirit gave better results. Barok, one of her great enemies in the profession berated her for this, claiming it broke tradition. She did not care about tradition though, she always sought the best results.

When she was done she applied a poultice. This also helped to fight infection, but its main purpose was to promote quicker healing and the drawing together of the edges of the wound.

If there was no sign of infection in several days, she would consider stitching it together. But if she did that too early, then it was possible that puss could build up inside, and that made infections worse.

She applied a bandage over the poultice, and then she was done. Brand would live or die now by his own will, by the natural strength of his body.

Those who had held him down were two girls. For the first time Arell allowed herself the chance to look around. One was an ash-blond woman, fierce and keen-eyed. The other … the other must have been one of the immortals, a Halathrin. And she seemed as sweet as a summer's day, though there was steel in her also.

Brand had kept strange company outside of the city, and much had evidently happened to him. The Halathrin did not venture beyond their forest realm, at least not these days, and there must be quite a story to this. But one thing about the two girls was the same, and she felt a pang of jealousy: they each felt for Brand. Their worry and their fear for him were palpable things. It was something that Arell had often seen when treating patients – the frightened concern of those who loved them.

Whatever jealousy Arell felt, she suppressed it. It was not her way, and it would do no good. Besides, it was clear that Brand had touched their hearts in some way, and she could not hold that against them. Had he not done the same to her?

Nevertheless, the three of them eyed each other off. But it was the fierce looking one, the one with the shadow of past pain in her eyes, that surprised her by speaking.

"I'm Kareste, and you must be Arell. Brand has told me of you."

"I'm sure he has."

There was a flicker of a smile on Kareste's face. "He said you were a great healer, and I believe him. He will not die, of that I'm certain. You won't let him. But, I won't be here when he wakes up. Tell him," she paused, "tell him that I said goodbye. Tell him that I've much to think about and consider. And tell him this also. I'll be back. One day I'll appear again, unexpectedly, just as I did when we first met."

She looked fierce for a moment, and there truly was a shadow in her eyes, but it was more than past pain.

Arell nodded. This girl obviously had many issues to work through.

"I'll tell him."

Arell stood, and the two of them exchanged a stiff curtsey. Kareste was ready to leave, but her glance fell on Aranloth and she paused. A long time they looked at each other.

The lòhren bowed to her. It was a thing that Arell had not seen him do even for the king.

"Well have you chosen," he said when he straightened.

She smiled at him, and her face changed completely.

"Good was my guide, and good was he who sent him to my aid. For did you not know that we would meet?"

Aranloth shrugged. "Perhaps. I hoped. But nothing is certain."

She bowed and started to walk away, but not toward the city. Then she turned to face the lòhren again.

"Brand will live. The healer-girl will care for him, and she will see to it. Thank him for me."

"I will. And when you're ready, return to Lòrenta. Your staff is there, and it would be better in your hands than lying unused in a dusty chamber."

She looked at him and smiled again. It was a happy smile, but a sad smile too.

"I'm not sure the other lòhrens are ready for me."

"All the more reason to return."

Her smile flashed fiercely, and then she turned and left.

The days passed, and they were long. But the nights were longer, for the pain grew worse. Yet, day by day, night by night, under the steady ministrations of Arell, Brand grew stronger.

Within a week he was walking around and receiving visitors. There were many of those, and the catching up with old friends and the exchange of news and the storytelling of recent events filled many hours.

He missed Kareste, but he understood that she needed time alone. He missed Harly also, for once he was on the mend she had come to say goodbye.

"This city is no place for me," she had said. "I yearn for the wild lands, the lands of forest and grass, and the stars up above at night."

He understood that as well. He understood it better than most, for he was like her.

"Don't forget me," she said.

"Never," he answered.

"Nor will I let you, for I suspect we shall meet again."

"Really? Halathar is far away. It may be that even my wandering feet never reach there."

"Perhaps not. But my feet wander also. And one day, when you leave this place of stone, this swirling storm of hustle and bustle behind, look for me in the quiet wilderness."

"I will always look for you," he said. And then she and the remnant of her band were gone.

The king came to see him, and he shook his head and laughed at the fate of the diamond.

"Perhaps you were never meant to be wealthy."

"Maybe not, but I'm rich in other ways."

Gilhain nodded sagely at that, and then he returned the knife, the knife of his ancestors marked with the sign of Halathgar, that he had given to Brand once before when this had all begun.

"I will keep it, this time."

Taingern and Shorty came to see him also. One was quiet and reserved, the other rowdy and jovial. But whatever their manner, he felt their love. But even Shorty grew subdued when they spoke of the Durlin who had died protecting the king since Brand had left the city.

All the while Arell kept a close eye on him, and when he grew tired she chased the two visitors away in quick order. Shorty, however, winked at him slyly before he went through the doorway.

The days passed, and Brand grew stronger. He was well enough to return to his own room, even to resume duty as the Durlindrath again. But Arell did not allow either, and he did not argue.

Yet, one bright morning when the sun shone and the sky was clear, he felt restless. And he knew the cause of it.

He took up Aranloth's staff and diadem, that Arell had stored in a closet, and went looking for the lòhren.

Aranloth was not hard to find, and after speaking to several soldiers Brand tracked him down. He was atop the battlement, where he was said these days to spend much time gazing out at the empty space where the enemy had once camped below.

"Ah," the lòhren said without turning. "The day has come at last, Brand."

Brand stood beside him and looked out at the view. The ground was ripped and pockmarked. In places, the earth was scorched. Yet green shoots were rising up from the trampled earth, and in the distance the pinewoods around Lake Alithorin were so green as to appear almost black.

Brand leaned the staff against the stone and put down the diadem.

"Why not tell me that you knew?"

Aranloth turned to look at him. "You know the answer to that."

Brand let out a long sigh and nodded.

The lòhren looked him steadily in the eye. "In the staff, that long I have born, since before the fall of the Letharn empire, there is only the memory of enchantment. The diadem, however, is different. If you better knew its history, you would better understand its virtue."

"So, what now?" Brand asked.

Aranloth turned his gaze back out to the empty countryside.

"You feel the call of the land, do you not? And in her voice are the dreams and hopes of all who would live in Alithoras, of all who would not succumb to the shadow of the south. Can you deny her?"

Brand shook his head.

"The land knows you well," Aranloth said. "The land from which you came, to which you will one day return. No servitude is it to serve her. She lays no bonds upon you. Yet bonds there are, for you lay them upon yourself. Do you accept this?"

Brand looked at the land below. Alithoras stretched out all around him, and though he could only see this small bit of it, he felt the rest.

"I will serve," he answered. "I will become a lòhren."

Aranloth did not answer, and after a moment Brand spoke again. This time, his voice was soft, barely more than a whisper, and the words he chanted were ones that he had long held dear.

174

Tum del conar – El dar tum.
Death or infamy – I choose death.

"I had thought," he added, "that those words only applied to serving the king. But they hold true for other things as well. They hold true for serving the whole land, and not just a part of it. They hold true for serving, and protecting, all who live in it."

Aranloth seemed surprised. "Yes," he said eventually. "They're fitting words for a lòhren as much as for a Durlin. More fitting than you could ever guess. For though you have no way of knowing this, they were uttered long ago, long before the Durlin existed, long before the Camar came east. Once, they were spoken in the very halls from whence you brought forth the second half of Shurilgar's staff, and the sound of them was like a death-knell to an entire empire."

Aranloth looked out over the battlement, but Brand knew the lòhren's eyes saw nothing. His mind was on some event, some recollection of so long ago, so world-shattering in its way that even its distant memory moved him in a manner that Brand could not understand.

"Strange, very strange that you should speak those words now, speak them in the context of a lòhren and not a Durlin. And all the more now do I feel that this is the right path for you."

Brand was not so sure of things. "What will be, will be," he said.

The lòhren's mood suddenly shifted, and he laughed. "You of all people don't believe that. You, who have foretellings hanging over your head wherever you go, and ignore them all."

Brand shrugged, but did not answer. He wondered just who, or what, Aranloth saw when he looked at him.

175

And Aranloth did look at him now, his mood changing again to one of warning.

"Remember this, and remember it always. You are now a lòhren, though you have much yet to learn. But your serving may take a different form than you think. Even to those who wander the paths of the future, its ways and its twists and turns are often unseen. Remember that in the days ahead."

Brand looked at him, looked at his oldest friend in Cardoroth, and felt the full force of those words. Aranloth knew something. And Brand had a feeling that the future held surprises for him. He smiled to himself, for it was a feeling that he liked.

Epilogue

A breeze touched the tops of the pine trees. Dusk was drawing close, and in the forest darkness had already descended, deep and impenetrable. Thus it always was in the woods that surrounded Lake Alithorin, and thus it would always remain.

Beneath the fringe of that forest, atop a hill, several pairs of eyes looked down coldly at what they saw. The landscape shone eerily under the slanting rays of the dying sun. The light flickered, shifted and changed as it danced to the movement of the cloud-wreck on the horizon, the remnant of the terrible storm. Those clouds, fired red by the lowering sun, seemed like blood poured across the western sky.

But redder still was the great wall of Cardoroth. Blood was on it, and it reeked of death. Blood was soaked into the soil, and the remembered screams of the dying hung in the air, though all that could be heard by the ears of the watchers was the rustle of pine leaves and the sounds of small animals scurrying in the shadows, hunter and hunted, playing their own battle of life and death. Those creatures recked nothing of men, thought nothing of the battles that had been fought. And they cared even less.

But the eyes that watched, or rather the minds that directed them, cared and understood. And they felt the joy of the city and the people who lived there, and it chagrined them. And they felt the terror of the fleeing elugs, and though that excited them, it disturbed them more.

One of the great masters had fallen, and there were few in the world like him. Just how it had happened, they did not know, but one of them sensed the involvement of Brand. Brand of the Duthenor come west into lands that had nothing to do with him, come west into lands to kill and destroy.

The death of Khamdar was a great event in Alithoras, yet it was a small thing beside the death of one other that Brand had killed.

Ginsar stared out through the falling night. She paid no heed to the cold glinting of the stars that sparked to life like far-away campfires in the dark sky. She thought nothing of the forest behind her, though it had been her home for years beyond the count of mortal men. She thought of nothing but Brand, and the more she thought, the greater the cold fury that burned within her grew.

"The battle is lost," she said to her three companions. "Khamdar underestimated Brand. That is a mistake I will not make, for I am not of the south as was Khamdar, and I have watched Brand closely over the years – and I have learned."

One of the black-cloaked elùgroths next to her spoke, and his voice was wary, for he had seen this mood on his leader before.

"But Mistress," he said, "if the battle is lost how can you attain revenge on Brand? He is safe in the walls of the city."

Ginsar turned to look at him, and her expression was cold, colder than the void in which the stars burned out their life surrounded by oblivion.

"I am Ginsar, and my power is great. Khamdar failed, but I will not, and the death of Brand will atone for my brother whom he killed. And for all Khamdar's power, he could not foretell the future as do I."

"And what do you see, Mistress?"

She looked back at Cardoroth, and a smile touched her lips, but it was colder than the black void.

"Brand thinks that soon he can leave the city, that his duty here is done. But that is not so. His duty will pin him here, like an insect crawling over stone and squashed beneath a booted foot. And that will be the death of him."

There was a pause, marked only by the rustle of the breeze through pine needles.

"How so, Mistress?" one of the other elùgroths asked after a moment.

Ginsar stood, silent as a stone, and whatever thoughts and plans spun through her mind, nothing showed on her face.

"This much I will reveal to you. The way to Brand is through those he loves. And one that he loves most will place a burden on him, and the care of a child."

There was another pause. She said nothing, and the elùgroths grew anxious.

She turned to them and grinned, and power was in her glance, unwavering and potent. But there was madness in it also. This the elùgroths recognized, but it mattered not. She led, and they followed. Thus it had ever been, even with her as it was with her brother, the master that they had served before they had taken her as mistress.

"The child is the key," she said. "I will use him to lure Brand to his downfall. And never will one have fallen from such heights to such depths. Never will one know such pain and regret. And I will draw it out, and savor every moment though it be unendurable torment to him."

"And what of the child himself?"

"Ah. The child. Such sweet revenge, for with him I can condemn Brand. Yet the child is also an enemy. Verily, that youth is born of the line of she that we hate most in all the world."

The elùgroths pondered this. After several moments and secret glances among themselves, one spoke.

179

"Mistress? Who is it that we hate even more than Brand?"

She looked at him coolly, and he trembled.

"Think, O fool. Think!"

One of the other elùgroths bowed, and glanced slyly at his discomforted brother. "Mistress. She that we hate is Carnhaina, and the child must be descended from that ancient witch."

Ginsar tossed back her long hair, black as the shadows of the forest. It was a girlish gesture, and, coming from her, was so out of place that it unnerved even the elùgroths.

"So he is, and destroying the boy and Brand together is fitting beyond description. For though the witch has been dead many centuries, still does her spirit linger in the city, watching and helping. And the destruction of Brand and the witch's descendant will drive my revenge deep into her long-dead heart, and her anguish will add to my ecstasy."

The stars wheeled above. The night wore on, and Ginsar revealed her plans to the elùgroths. And even they, dark souls though they were, blanched.

Thus ends *Victorious Swords*. It brings the Durlindrath series to a conclusion. Yet the growing power of the south, and the madness of Ginsar, imperils all of Alithoras and more of the desperate struggle will soon be told.

Sign up below and be the first to hear about new book releases, see previews and learn of upcoming discounts. http://eepurl.com/Rswv1

Visit my website at www.homeofhighfantasy.com

Encyclopedic Glossary

Note: the glossary of each book in this series is individualized for that book alone. Additionally, there is often historical material provided in its entries for people, artifacts and events that are not included in the main text.

Many races dwell in Alithoras. All have their own language, and though sometimes related to one another, the changes sparked by migration, isolation and various influences often render these tongues unintelligible to each other.

The ascendancy of Halathrin culture, combined with their widespread efforts to secure and maintain allies against elug incursions, has made their language the primary means of communication between diverse peoples.

For instance, a soldier of Cardoroth addressing a ship's captain from Camarelon would speak Halathrin, or a simplified version of it, even though their native speeches stem from the same ancestral language.

This glossary contains a range of names and terms. Many are of Halathrin origin, and their meaning is provided. The remainder derive from native tongues and are obscure, so meanings are only given intermittently.

Some variation exists within the Halathrin language, chiefly between the regions of Halathar and Alonin. The most obvious example is the latter's preference for a "dh" spelling instead of "th".

Often, Camar names and Halathrin elements are combined. This is especially so for the aristocracy. No other tribes had such long-term friendship with the Halathrin, and though in this relationship they lost some of their natural culture, they gained nobility and knowledge in return.

List of abbreviations:

Azn. Azan

Cam. Camar

Chg. Cheng

Comb. Combined

Cor. Corrupted form

Duth. Duthenor

Esg. Esgallien

Hal. Halathrin

Leth. Letharn

Prn. Pronounced

Age of heroes: A period of Camar history that has become mythical. Many tales are told of this time. Some are true, others are not. And yet, even the false ones usually contain elements of historical fact. Many were the heroes who walked abroad during this time, and they are remembered still, and honored still, by the Camar people. The old days are looked back on with pride, and the descendants of many heroes yet walk the streets of Cardoroth, though they be unaware of their heritage and the accomplishments of their forefathers.

Alar: *Azn.* A strain of horses raised in the southern deserts of Alithoras. Bred for endurance, but capable of bursts of speed. Most valued possession of the Azan people, who measure wealth and status by their number. In their culture, where a person on foot is likely to die between water sources, horse-theft is punished by torture and death.

Alithoras: *Hal.* "Silver land." The Halathrin name for the continent they settled after the exodus. Refers to the extensive river and lake systems they found and their appreciation of the beauty of the land.

Alith Nien: *Hal.* "Silver river." Has its source in the mountainous lands of Auren Dennath and empties into Lake Alithorin.

Anast Dennath: *Hal.* "Stone mountains." Mountain range in northern Alithoras. Contiguous with Auren Dennath and location of the Dweorhrealm.

Angle: The land hemmed in by the Carist Nien and Erenian rivers, especially the area in proximity to their divergence.

Angrod: One of the ancient names of the witch better known in present times as Durletha.

Arach Neben: *Hal.* "West gate." The great wall surrounding Cardoroth has four gates. Each is named after a cardinal direction, and each also carries a token to represent a celestial object. Arach Neben bears a steel ornament of the Morning Star.

Aranloth: *Hal.* "Noble might." A lòhren.

Arell: A name formerly common among the Camar people, but currently out of favor in Cardoroth. Its etymology is obscure, though it is speculated that it derives from the Halathrin stems "aran" and "ell" meaning noble and slender. Ell, in the Halathrin tongue, also refers to any type of timber that is pliable, for instance, hazel. This is cognate with our word wych-wood, meaning timber that is supple and pliable. As elùgroths use wych-wood staffs as instruments of sorcery, it is sometimes supposed that their name derives from this stem, rather than elù (shadowed). This is a viable philological theory. Nevertheless, as a matter of historical fact, it is wrong.

Aurellin: *Cor. Hal.* The first element means blue. The second appears to be native Camar. Queen of Cardoroth and wife to Gilhain.

Auren Dennath: *Comb. Duth.* and *Hal. Prn.* Our-ren dennath. "Blue mountains." Mountain range in northern Alithoras. Contiguous with Anast Dennath.

Azan: *Azn.* Desert dwelling people. Their nobility often serve as leaders of elug armies. They are a prideful race, often haughty and domineering, but they also adhere to a strict code of honor.

185

Barok: A healer in Cardoroth. A man held in high regard by the profession he represents. Distantly related to the king on his mother's side. It is believed by some that he obtained his position as chief physician via political influence. Others argue that, his family being wealthy, they bribed the king's chancellor in order to obtain the favored position for one of their own. Be that as it may, it is well known in Gilhain's court that the king dislikes him. This likely stems from an older cause, however. In his youth, the king required stitches. Barok inserted them, but miscalculated the date of their removal. The process, undertaken many days later than it should have been, was painful. Gilhain still bears the scars on his arm, not just of the initial cut, but also the faint point marks where the string was pulled from his flesh.

Black Corps: An irregular unit of cavalry for Cardoroth. Formed by direct command of the king. Its leader, Hilk Var Jernik, was appointed its captain after the king had seen him ride in a competition. At that time, he was of low rank in the regular cavalry. His officers commended him, but said he was willful and unsuited to command. The king researched his military exploits, overruled the commanders, and ensured the Black Corps answered directly to the throne rather than the leadership of the regular cavalry.

Brand: A Duthenor tribesman. Currently serving King Gilhain as his Durlindrath. By birth, he is the rightful chieftain of the Duthenor people. However, an usurper overthrew his father, killing him and his wife. Brand, only a youth at the time, swore an oath of vengeance. That oath sleeps, but it is not forgotten, either by Brand or the usurper. The usurper sought to have him killed also, but without success.

Camar: *Cam. Prn.* Kay-mar. A race of interrelated tribes that migrated in two main stages. The first brought them to the vicinity of Halathar; in the second, they separated and established cities along a broad sweep of eastern Alithoras.

Camarelon: *Cam. Prn.* Kam-arelon. A port city and capital of a Camar tribe. It was founded before Cardoroth as the waves of migrating people settled the more southerly lands first. Each new migration tended northward. It is perhaps the most representative of a traditional Camar realm.

Cardoroth: *Cor. Hal. Comb. Cam.* A Camar city, often called Red Cardoroth. Some say this alludes to the red granite commonly used in the construction of its buildings, others that it refers to a prophecy of destruction.

Cardurleth: *Hal.* "Car – red, dur – steadfast, leth – stone." The great wall that surrounds Cardoroth. Established soon after the city's founding and constructed with red granite. It looks displeasing to the eye, but the people of the city love it nonetheless. They believe it impregnable and say that no enemy shall ever breach it – except by treachery.

Careth Nien: *Hal. Prn.* Kareth nyen. "Great river." Largest river in Alithoras. Has its source in the mountains of Anast Dennath and runs southeast across the land before emptying into the sea. It was over this river (which sometimes freezes along its northern stretches) that the

Camar and other tribes migrated into the eastern lands. Much later, Brand came to the city of Cardoroth by one of these ancient migratory routes.

Carist Nien: *Hal.* "Ice river." A river of northern Alithoras that has its source in the hills of Lòrenta.

Carnhaina: First element native *Cam.* Second *Hal.* "Heroine." An ancient queen of Cardoroth. Revered as a savior of her people, but to some degree also feared, for she possessed powers of magic. Hated to this day by elùgroths, because she overthrew their power unexpectedly at a time when their dark influence was rising. According to dim legend, kept alive mostly within the royal family of Cardoroth, she guards the city even in death and will return in its darkest hour.

Carnyx horn: The sacred horn of the Camar tribes. An instrument of brass, man high with a mouth fashioned in the likeness of a fierce animal, often a boar or bear. Winded in battle and designed to intimidate the foe with its otherworldly sound. Some believe it invokes supernatural aid.

Chapterhouse: Special halls set aside in the palace of Cardoroth for the private meetings, teachings and military training of the Durlin.

Crenel: The vertical gap on a battlement between merlons. The merlon offers protection, the crenel an opening through which missiles are fired.

Drilk: Lieutenant in the Black Corps and second in command to Jar Van Hilk. Married to Jar's sister. Their extended family operates a horse stud that produces mounts not just for the Black Corps, but also the regular cavalry of Cardoroth. The leaders of the regular cavalry often complain to the king that the best horses are held back from sale. The king advises them to make better bids at the auctions.

Drinhalath: *Hal.* "Drin – a group of people united in one purpose, Halath – a long-dead Halathrin king." The Drinhalath is an order chosen by the living king from the people as a reward or honor for some great service or deed to the people. The service itself, of protecting the remains of the memorial, lasts for twenty years.

Drùghoth: *Hal.* First element – black. Second element – that which hastens, races or glides. More commonly called a sending.

Drùgluck: A pattern of three slanted lines, going from right to left and each one longer than the previous. Used by elugs as a warning to stay away from a place because it is a sacred area that serves as a gateway between the spirit and normal worlds. Such areas are used in ceremonies and invocations for help or retribution against enemies. It is believed that at certain cycles of the moon and seasons the barriers that separate the worlds are weakened and the gateway opens. Also marks a place where the effects of elùgai linger or where there is some unspecified but lethal danger. Often it signifies all three at once.

Durletha: *Hal.* "She who is as enduring as stone." A witch of Alithoras whose birth was before even the rise of the ancient, but now forgotten, Letharn empire.

Durlin: *Hal.* "The steadfast." The original Durlin were the seven sons of the first king of Cardoroth. They guarded him against all enemies, of which there were many, and three died to protect him. Their tradition continued throughout Cardoroth's history, suspended only once, and briefly, some four hundred years ago when it was discovered that three members were secretly in the service of elùgroths. These were imprisoned, but committed suicide while waiting for the king's trial to commence. It is rumored that the king himself provided them with the knives that they used. It is said that he felt sorry for them and gave them this way out to avoid the shame a trial would bring to their families.

Durlin creed: These are the native Camar words, long remembered and much honored, uttered by the first Durlin to die while he defended his father, and king, from attack. Tum del conar – El dar tum! Death or infamy – I choose death! This man was a pupil of the lòhren Aranloth.

Durlindrath: *Hal.* "Lord of the steadfast." The title given to the leader of the Durlin.

Duthenor: *Duth. Prn.* Dooth-en-or. "The people." A single tribe, or sometimes a group of tribes melded into a larger people at times of war or disaster, who generally live a rustic and peaceful lifestyle. They are raisers of cattle and herders of sheep. However, when need demands they are fierce warriors – men and women alike.

Eleth nar duril: *Hal.* "Lie in peace." Part of the Halathrin funerary chant.

Elugs: *Hal.* "That which creeps in shadows." A cruel and superstitious race that inhabits the southern lands, especially the Graèglin Dennath.

190

Elùdrath: *Hal. Prn.* Eloo-drath. "Shadowed lord." A sorcerer. First and greatest among elùgroths. Believed to be dead or defeated.

Elùgai: *Hal. Prn.* Eloo-guy. "Shadowed force." The sorcery of an elùgroth.

Elùgroth: *Hal. Prn.* Eloo-groth. "Shadowed horror." A sorcerer. They often take names in the Halathrin tongue in mockery of the lòhren's practice to do so.

Elu-haraken: *Hal.* "The shadowed wars." Long ago battles in a time that is become myth to the Camar tribes.

Exodus: The arrival of the Halathrin into Alithoras from an outside land. They came by ship and beached north of Anast Dennath.

Foresight: Premonition of the future. Can occur at random as a single image or as a longer sequence of events. Can also be deliberately sought by entering the realm between life and death where the spirit is released from the body to travel through space and time. To achieve this, the body must be brought to the very threshold of death. The first method is uncontrollable and rare. The second exceedingly rare but controllable for those with the skill and willingness to endure the danger.

Forgotten Queen (the): An epithet for Queen Carnhaina.

Free Cities: A group of cooperative city states that pool military resources to defend themselves against attack. Founded prior to Cardoroth. Initially ruled by kings and queens, now by a senate.

Galenthern: *Hal.* "Green flat." Southern plains bounded by the Careth Nien and the Graèglin Dennath mountain range.

Gavnor: A lòhren of Queen Carnhaina's ancient court. Driven by desperate need he attempted to Spirit Walk, though he did not have sufficient skill. He saw deeply into what was, and what yet may be. But he was assailed. He had neither the skill to attempt to defend himself, nor to return to his body. He was lost in the void, from whence none had ever returned. Yet Carnhaina recalled him, revealing herself as a great power, greater than most lòhrens or elùgroths. But Gavnor was changed by the experience. He withdrew from the court, renounced his stature among the lòhren order, and wandered the land as a lover of nature. It is said that his power was increased, and he may well yet still live. But none have seen him for long centuries.

Gernlik: *Cam.* A Durlin.

Gilhain: *Comb. Cam & Hal.* First element unknown, second "hero." King of Cardoroth. Husband to Aurellin.

Graèglin Dennath: *Hal. Prn.* Greg-lin dennath. "Mountains of ash." Chain of mountains in southern Alithoras. The landscape is one of jagged stone and boulder, relieved only by gaping fissures from which plumes of ashen smoke ascend, thus leading to its name. Believed to be impassable because of the danger of poisonous air flowing from cracks, and the ground unexpectedly giving way, swallowing any who dare to tread its forbidden paths. In other places swathes of molten stone run in rivers down its slopes.

Great North Road: An ancient construction of the Halathrin. Built at a time when they had settlements in the northern reaches of Alithoras. Warriors traveled swiftly from north to south in order to aid the main population who dwelt in Halathar when they faced attack from the south.

Grothanon: *Hal.* "Horror desert." The flat salt plains south of the Graèglin Dennath.

Halath: *Hal.* King of the Halathrin. He died thousands of years ago. He led them on their exodus to Alithoras. Revered and loved as a great ruler. Originally, one of the main opponents of Elùdrath, leader of the elùgroths who sought dominion over Alithoras.

Halathar: *Hal.* "Dwelling place of the people of Halath." The forest realm of the Halathrin.

Halathgar: *Hal.* "Bright star." Actually a constellation. Also known as the Lost Huntress.

Halathrin: *Hal.* "People of Halath." A race named after a mighty lord who led an exodus of his people to the continent of Alithoras in pursuit of justice, having sworn to redress a great evil. They are human, though of fairer form, greater skill and higher culture than ordinary men. They possess an inherent unity of body, mind and spirit enabling insight and endurance beyond other races of Alithoras. Reported to be immortal, but killed in great numbers during their conflicts with the evil they seek to destroy. Those conflicts are collectively known as the elù-haraken: the Shadowed Wars.

Harlak: *Leth.* An ancient name of Aranloth.

Harath Neben: *Hal.* "North gate." This gate bears a token of two massive emeralds that represent the constellation of Halathgar. The gate is also known as "Hunter's Gate," for the north road out of the city leads to wild lands full of game.

Harlinlanloth: *Hal.* "The mighty power of gentle water over long years." Current leader of the Drinhalath. Puissant in a form of Halathrin magic.

Harly: See Harlinlanloth.

Hilk Var Jernik: Captain of the Black Corps. A man of rare courage, intellect and judgement. Sentenced to a year's servitude into the army of Cardoroth after being convicted of theft in his youth. So much did he impress his superior officers that they recommended him for promotion. This was denied by the aristocratic leaders of the army. The king, however, saw his worth as a man and promoted him.

Hvargil: Prince of Cardoroth. Younger son of Carangil, former king of Cardoroth. Exiled by Carangil for treason after it was discovered he plotted with elùgroths to assassinate his older half-brother, Gilhain, and prevent him from one day ascending to the throne. He gathered a band about him in exile of outlaws and discontents. Most came from Cardoroth but others were drawn from Camarelon.

Immortals: See Halathrin.

Jinks: See Hilk Var Jernik.

Karappe: A great healer of antiquity. Responsible for many of the medical treatises still used today among the

Camar peoples. He lived to 109 years of age, and remained sprightly well past his hundredth birthday. Famous for recommending two mugs of beer, or one glass of wine, a day as good for health.

Kareste: A mysterious girl who helps Brand. She possess potent magic.

Kardoch: A hero of ancient lethrin society. Revered by them, and at times worshipped by them. It is believed that the elùgroths stamp out the latter practice. They have no room in their rule for reverence of anything save their own power, and the power that they ultimately serve themselves.

Khamdar: An elùgroth. Leader of the host the besieges Cardoroth.

Kirsch: A race of men who established a mighty empire across Alithoras. Yet they predated even the Letharn and nearly all knowledge of them is lost forever.

Lake Alithorin: *Hal.* "Silver lake." A lake of northern Alithoras.

Letharn: *Hal.* "Stone raisers. Builders." A race of people that in antiquity ruled much of Alithoras. Only traces of their civilization remain.

Lethrin: *Hal.* "Stone people." Creatures of the Graèglin Dennath. Renowned for their size and strength. Tunnelers and miners.

Limloth: Hal. "Still-peace." The "loth" element is the same stem as appears in Aranloth's name. However, in this context it means a powerful or mighty sense of tranquility, a sense of serenity that has a prevailing effect on a person rather than as a force to achieve some physical impact. The name refers to an especially peaceful area in a high and remote section of the Auren Dennath mountain range.

Lòhren: *Hal. Prn.* Ler-ren. "Knowledge giver – a counsellor." Other terms used by various nations include wizard, druid and sage.

Lòhren-fire: A defensive manifestation of lòhrengai. The color of the flame varies according to the skill and temperament of the lòhren.

Lòhrengai: *Hal. Prn.* Ler-ren-guy. "Lòhren force." Enchantment, spell or use of arcane power. A manipulation and transformation of the natural energy inherent in all things. Each use takes something from the user. Likewise, some part of the transformed energy infuses them. Lòhrens use it sparingly, elùgroths indiscriminately.

Lòhrenin: *Hal. Prn.* Ler-ren-in. "Council of lòhrens."

Lòrenta: *Hal. Prn.* Ler-rent-a. "Hills of knowledge." Uplands in northern Alithoras in which the stronghold of the lòhrens is established.

Lornach: A Durlin. Friend to Brand and often called by his nickname of "Shorty."

Lost Huntress: See Halathgar.

Magic: Supernatural power. See lòhrengai and elùgai.

Merlon: The vertical stonework on a battlement between crenels. The merlon offers protection, the crenel a gap through which missiles are fired.

Narinon: *Hal.* "Spear-water, a swimmer or diver." A member of the Drinhalath. In love with Harlinlanloth, though aware that his feelings are not returned. Bears a facial scar due to a fight with a lethrin in an ancient battle. The lethrin did not survive, but his dying stroke nearly killed the Halathrin warrior.

Netherwall: One of the ancient names of the witch better known in present times as Durletha.

Nudaluk: *Cam.* A bird of the woodpecker family.

Otherworld: Camar term for a mingling of half-remembered history, myth and the spirit world.

Raithlin: *Hal.* "Range and report people." A scouting and saboteur organization. In Camar society, they derive from ancient contact with, and the teachings of, the Halathrin. In Halathrin history the roots of the order predate the exodus.

Red-fletched arrows: Cardoroth is famed for having great archers, and the greatest of them always use the red feathers of the Cara-hak turkey for their fletching. The bird is revered by them as a creature of luck, and it is considered ill fortune to shoot one. But many a farmer or hungry hunter does so, and the feathers are never wasted. But a wide variety of feathers are used from different bird species for arrow making, though all are dyed red before use.

Sellic Neben: *Hal.* "East gate." This gate bears a representation, crafted of silver and pearl, of the moon rising over the sea.

Sending: See Drùghoth.

Shadowed Lord: See Elùdrath.

Shazrahad: The Azan who commands an elug army, or serves as a lieutenant of an elùgroth.

Shorty: See Lornach.

Shurilgar: *Hal.* "Midnight star." An elùgroth. Also called the betrayer of nations.

Sight: The ability to discern the intentions and even thoughts of another person. Not reliable, and yet effective at times.

Slithrest: One of the ancient names of the witch better known in present times as Durletha.

Spirit walk: Similar in process to foresight. It is deliberately sought by entering the realm between life and death where the spirit is released from the body to travel through space. To achieve this, the body must be brought to the very threshold of death. This is exceedingly dangerous and only attempted by those of paramount skill.

Sorcerer: See Elùgroth.

Sorcery: See elùgai.

Surcoat: An outer garment. Often worn over chain mail. The Durlin surcoat is unadorned white.

Taingern: *Cam*. A Durlin. Friend to Brand.

Tombs of the Letharn: The ancient burial place of the Letharn people. All members of the population, throughout the course of their long civilization, were laid to rest here. It was believed that to be interred elsewhere was to condemn the spirit to a true death, rather than an afterlife. The dead were preserved, and returned even from the far reaches of the empire. This was withheld from perpetrators of treason and heinous crimes. These were buried in special cemeteries near the river. Petty criminals were afforded an opportunity to redeem their place in the tombs on payment of a fine determined by the head-priest.

Tower of Halathgar: In life, the place of study of Queen Carnhaina. In death, her resting place. Somewhat unusually, her sarcophagus rests on the tower's parapet beneath the stars.

Unlach Neben: *Hal.* "South gate." This gate bears a representation of the sun, crafted of gold, beating down upon a desert land. Said by some to signify the homeland of the elugs, whence the gold of the sun was obtained by an adventurer of old.

War drums: Drums of the elug tribes. Used especially in times of war or ceremony. Rumored to carry hidden messages in their beat and also to invoke sorcery.

Wizard: See lòhren.

Wych-wood: A general description for a range of supple and springy timbers. Some hardy varieties are prevalent on the poisonous slopes of the Graèglin Dennath mountain range and are favored by elùgroths as instruments of sorcery.

From the author

I'm a man born in the wrong era. My heart yearns for faraway places and even further afield times. Tolkien had me at the beginning of *The Hobbit* when he said, ". . . one morning long ago in the quiet of the world . . ."

Sometimes I imagine myself in a Viking mead-hall. The long winter night presses in, but the shimmering embers of a log in the hearth hold back both cold and dark. The chieftain calls for a story, and I take a sip from my drinking horn and stand up . . .

Or maybe the desert stars shine bright and clear, obscured occasionally by wisps of smoke from burning camel dung. A dry gust of wind marches sand grains across our lonely campsite, and the wayfarers about me stir restlessly. I sip cool water and begin to speak.

I'm a storyteller. A man to paint a picture by the slow music of words. I like to bring faraway places and times to life, to make hearts yearn for something they can never have, unless for a passing moment.